BY MATT FORBECK

RETURN OF
THE PIGLINS

RETURN OF THE PIGLINS

MATT FORBECK

RANDOM HOUSE WORLDS

NEW YORK

Copyright © 2023 Mojang AB. All Rights Reserved. Minecraft, the
MINECRAFT logo, the MOJANG STUDIOS logo, and the CREEPER logo
are trademarks of the Microsoft group of companies.

Published in the United States by Random House Worlds,
an imprint of Random House, a division of
Penguin Random House LLC, New York.

RANDOM HOUSE is a registered trademark,
and RANDOM HOUSE WORLDS and colophon
are trademarks of Penguin Random House LLC.

Hardback ISBN 978-0-593-35571-8
International edition ISBN 978-0-593-72412-5
Ebook ISBN 978-0-593-35572-5

Endpapers: M. S. Corley

Printed in the United States of America on acid-free paper

randomhousebooks.com

2 4 6 8 9 7 5 3 1

First Edition

Book design by Elizabeth A. D. Eno

For Ann, Marty, Laura, Pat, Nick, Ken, and Helen, who always show me how to have the most fun

MINECRAFT™
Legends

RETURN OF
THE PIGLINS

PROLOGUE

"**W**here is Kritten?" The Great Bungus's bellow echoed throughout the crude throne room of their crumbling piglin bastion. "I need their smarts, and I need them now!"

As the leader of perhaps the largest—and arguably the most powerful—clan of piglins in the entire Nether, Bungus liked to make demands and to have them answered instantly. They hadn't fought their way to the top of this heap to have people ignore their demands, no matter how ridiculous they might be. The fact that Kritten seemed to be avoiding them once again—if not outright hiding from their entirely righteous wrath—made their blood boil like the lakes of lava that bubbled through the bastion's broken walls.

"You don't need them!" Uggub grunted. "You got me!"

Bungus side-eyed the massive piglin brute. "You're not smart! Just strong! The kind of trouble we got now, muscles can't help with. We need smarts to fix it! Kritten's smarts!"

Uggub grunted louder, huffing with indignity at the idea that sheer brawn wasn't the solution to every issue. "Muscle got you this bastion! Muscle can keep it!"

Bungus leaped up from the rough stone throne and backhanded Uggub across the floor. "Did your muscle stop that? Huh?"

Uggub wiped their jaw clean as they pushed to their feet. They glared at Bungus as if their eyes could shoot arrows straight through the piglin boss's head.

Bungus snorted at Uggub. "There's too much out there in the Nether that can kill us! Too many other piglins who want what we got! Muscle's not enough to stop it! The walls of this bastion can't last against it all either! It's too much! We need smarts!"

Hearing how much Bungus needed their help, Kritten decided it might be worth risking their wrath. The much smaller piglin adjusted their robes, slipped out of their hiding space behind Bungus's throne, and leaped into the light shining down through the battered bastion's broken roof.

"I got smarts!" Kritten said, their voice bright and hopeful and only quivering with the faintest bit of fear. "I got just the kind of smarts you need, right here in my head! I can help!"

Bungus spun around and backhanded the overeager piglin in the other direction. Kritten—who was less than half the size of the towering Bungus and Uggub—rolled away like a chewed-up skull until they smacked into the room's far wall. They lay there stunned for a moment at the mostly unexpected reversal of fortune.

Kritten shook their head clear. "What did I do?"

Bungus stalked toward them, thick hands squeezed into massive fists. "That's not what's wrong! The trouble is what you *didn't* do!"

Kritten cowered as the long shadow of their leader loomed over them. "I've been trying! You know I've been trying!"

"Trying is not good enough!" Bungus stomped their booted foot. "I might try not to squash you! I might fail at that too!"

"I helped you take over this bastion!" Kritten shouted up at Bungus, terrified but somehow still defiant. "I help you keep it!"

"You try to help us keep it!" Uggub snorted. "If we fail at that, some other piglins will take it from us!"

Bungus gasped at the idea that Uggub had finally given voice to: the thought that Bungus's clan had grown so weak that some other piglin clan might be able to kick them out of the bastion — or worse!

It would only be fair, thought Kritten. *That's how Bungus got this bastion, after all.*

"Never!" Bungus thundered at Uggub. "That will never happen! We will not let it!"

Uggub snorted dismissively. "That's what Grungert said too — before you took the bastion from them! This is the piglin way! We take until we are taken!"

Bungus refused to accept any of that. "Not this time! Not from us! Not from me!"

Uggub snuffled at the slightly larger piglin. "What makes you so different?" Kritten could see the seeds of betrayal already growing in the brute's thick skull.

Bungus stabbed a scarred and meaty finger at Kritten. "Because the smart one here will stop it! They will find a way to protect us! To keep this bastion for us!"

"Us?" Kritten shook their head, wondering if the traitorous thoughts growing in Uggub's head had begun to infect their own mind too. "You mean you!"

Bungus chuckled. "This is not about me anymore! Not *just* about me! It's about *us*!"

Uggub's brow creased as the brute struggled to understand Bungus's line of reasoning. The brute wasn't particularly practiced at thinking. "How do you figure?"

"If I fall, the clan falls with me. We don't have enough piglins to defend this place without me! Not anymore! And when we don't have enough piglins—!"

Kritten finished the boss's sentence in a much quieter voice. "The other piglin clans will charge in and destroy whoever's left."

Despite how soft Kritten's voice had become, those words echoed through the otherwise utterly silent throne room.

Even Uggub realized that Kritten was right—but that only made the brute madder. They turned toward the smaller piglin, their face contorted with rage. "So what are you going to do about it, smart one?"

Kritten froze, their eyes darting toward the throne room's only exit. A pair of well-armed piglin guards stood just outside of it, pretending that they hadn't heard the entire conversation. Kritten would never make it past them.

Cornered, Kritten leaped to their feet instead and squared off against Bungus, doing their level best not to tremble in fear—and failing at that too. The best they could hope for was that the way they were shaking might come across as rage. "You think I haven't been trying? I'm doing everything I can! It's not my fault!"

Bungus advanced toward Kritten, and the advisor hastened to clarify themself. "It's not even yours! I studied what happened with the last five leaders in charge of this bastion, and none of them could stop this from happening either!"

Bungus stabbed Kritten in the chest with a thick finger, pressing the smaller piglin against the wall hard enough to make their heart hurt. "Maybe you're the problem! Maybe it's me! Either way, you got one last chance to fix this!"

"And if I don't?" Kritten was tired of taking abuse like this. They had worked alongside Bungus for a long time now, and it had been a good partnership, one that benefited them both. It had gotten them this bastion, something they'd been working toward for as long as Kritten could remember. But now that they'd achieved that, what would happen next?

Bungus drew a thumb across their throat and then jerked it over their shoulder. "Then you're out of here! Into the Nether! On your own!"

Kritten recoiled as far as the wall would allow, which wasn't much. "That's a death sentence! The hoglins out there will eat me alive!"

Bungus chortled. "Then at least you'd finally do some good for somebody!"

FOR THE ZOO

When it comes to being a zookeeper, I'm an absolute failure, Farnum thought as he hiked through the Overworld, glad that no one could hear him confessing what he really thought of himself. It was hard enough keeping up appearances around his friends so that they wouldn't abandon him. He just couldn't lie that well to himself.

The sun hung high in the nearly cloudless sky, shining down on Farnum and the rolling landscape that tumbled toward the mountain range just outside of the town he'd been born in and known all his life. All sorts of animals wandered around the place, grazing on the copious grass and swimming through the nearby river. He had studied them well and knew them all—perhaps a little too well.

It's too bad, then, that being a zookeeper is my job.

The trouble wasn't that Farnum disliked animals. When it came to the creatures in his zoo, he'd built habitats for them that were far better than anything they'd have found out in the wild. If they had to give up their freedom to roam anywhere, after all, it seemed only fair that he make their new homes as wonderful for them as he possibly could.

The trouble was that his zoo was small and only featured creatures like the ones he saw now on his hike: common and ordinary ones that anyone else could see in the wild by simply venturing outside the town limits on their own feet. The only thing the zoo offered any of its visitors was convenience.

Farnum knew this was his place's biggest flaw, but he didn't know what he could do about it. He'd never intended to open a zoo, but he'd somehow found himself in charge of one.

It had all started when he'd been out on a hike on a day very much like today and had stumbled across an injured fox. Such creatures were usually only found in taiga biomes, so it must have wandered far from its home. He normally never would have been able to capture such a creature with his bare hands, but hurt as it was, it had allowed him to gather it up in his arms and take it home so he could nurse it back to health.

Once Reynard—as he'd named the fox—was healthy again, Farnum had tried to release it into the wild again, but the fox hadn't wanted to go. It just stuck around his home and begged for sweet berries instead. Eventually Farnum had relented and taken the fox in. Rather than let it run wild in his house—where it kept picking up his things and carrying them about—he'd built a large enclosure for it outside of his place.

While the pen had been more to keep people out of the fox's designated area than to keep Reynard in, once people realized that there was a fox living in town they started coming around to get a better look at it. Someone eventually asked if they could make a donation to help pay for Reynard's upkeep, and it wasn't long after that Farnum decided to make the zoo an official thing and build it around Reynard's home.

Unfortunately, Farnum was terrible at finding rare and exotic creatures and bringing them back to the zoo. To date, the only other creatures in the zoo besides Reynard were a cow, a donkey, a pair of sheep, a rabbit, and a turtle—the kinds of creatures you could find all over the lands around town.

Perhaps not surprisingly, no one seemed to care much about them.

Despite that, Farnum had put a lot of effort into giving each of the creatures a wonderful home and keeping them fed and sheltered. He hadn't considered this as a business decision but as simply the right thing to do for these lost creatures, and he didn't have the heart to chase any of them out when they refused to leave.

Still, if they were going to stick around he felt obligated to feed them, and the donations for the zoo had mostly dried up. If he didn't get something new and exciting into the zoo soon, he'd have to start choosing between feeding the animals or feeding himself.

The thought made his stomach rumble. He adjusted the watertight pack on his back and wondered how long he could go before opening it up for a snack.

"At least it's a beautiful day," he said aloud to no one at all.

That's when he spotted the cave, or at least the opening into it: a wide hole tucked away under the edge of a rolling hill. The sight of it turned his blood cold.

Farnum had never traveled all that far from his hometown. Not since that incident in the Underworld, as he liked to call it, when he was young. He liked his hometown. It was comfortable and safe and full of all sorts of people he'd known forever. Other than wanting to find new animals for his zoo, he had never had a strong desire to leave.

Because he wanted to bring more—and more unusual—creatures into the zoo, though, he'd been striking out farther and farther on his hikes. He knew that finding really exotic creatures would mean having to explore much farther away, and he was working up to that. In the meantime, he figured scouring the lands around the town would make for a good start.

But did that really have to involve going into a cave? Couldn't he just stick to the surface, where he could see long distances and flee if anything dangerous came after him? A terrible experience he'd had as a youth had involved going underground, and he was not eager to repeat the experience.

Still, he told himself, *a cave's not really the Underworld, right? It's not like I have to dig to get into it. It's right there, open to the rest of the world.*

He wasn't sure he believed that, but his curiosity about what he might find in the cave warred with his fears—about what in the cave might find *him*.

Without him willing it, his feet drew him closer to the mouth of the cave. *It's okay to get closer. The sun is shining warm and bright out here. It's not like the Underworld can just reach out of the cave's mouth and grab me. Right?*

He did his best to agree with himself and crept closer and closer to the mouth of the cave, step by agonizing step. After what seemed like all day, he found himself standing at the cave's lip and staring into it.

Sunlight slanted down through the opening, illuminating the first several feet of the cave's rocky floor. Farnum couldn't make out much beyond that, other than to see that the cave was much larger than he had hoped. If he wanted to know what might live inside of it, he was going to have to enter it.

He just didn't know if he could make himself do that.

He broke out a torch and lit it, holding it high over his head as he edged forward. The cave, he found, stretched back farther than the torch would let him see. He cocked his head to one side and tried to listen as hard as he could for anything that might be living in the cave. All he could detect was a faint trickling of water somewhere in the distance.

He froze there, unable to force his feet to move forward, no matter how hard he tried. The sound of the beating of his heart in his chest grew louder and louder in his ears, drowning out anything else. The urge to turn around and run back home tugged at him so hard he didn't know how he could deny it.

Then he heard footsteps coming up behind him.

THE EXPEDITION

Farnum's first instinct was to run, but since the footsteps were coming from behind him, that would have meant charging into the cave. Still unable to bear the idea of plunging into the darkness, he spun around to confront whatever might be approaching him.

"Is that you, Farnum?" a familiar voice called out. "What in the Nether are you doing all the way out here?"

A laugh leaped from Farnum's throat. This wasn't a creeper, a skeleton, or some other creature coming up behind him—which they wouldn't have done in the daytime anyhow, but fear had made him foolish.

No, it was a friend! Someone he hadn't seen in far too long. "Grinchard! It's you!" Farnum's fears fell away as he dashed toward the explorer, fighting back tears of relief.

"Who else would it be, you fool?" Grinchard laughed as Farnum reached them and threw his arms around them.

The zookeeper was so relieved to see the explorer that he hadn't even noticed that someone else was there too.

"But he's not alone!" Mycra said, piping up from just behind Grinchard. She swept around his right side and joined in what had now become a group hug. "I'm so glad we found you!"

Farnum stepped back and smiled at them both, happy but confused. "Why were you looking for me?"

"I suppose that's my fault," Grinchard confessed. "I just got back in town from my latest adventure, and the first thing I wanted to do was see my pals again."

"So they stopped by and grabbed me," Mycra interrupted.

"And we went looking for you," Grinchard finished.

Farnum nodded, instantly understanding. "But I wasn't home!"

Grinchard chuckled. "No, you weren't! Which shocked me, of course, but didn't surprise Mycra much."

"I told them how worried you've been about your zoo," Mycra explained. "How you've been scouring the lands around here in the hopes of finding more creatures to bring into it."

Grinchard craned their neck around and gazed at the familiar landscape sprawling all around them. "You're going to have to get a lot farther away than this if you want to find anything really interesting."

Farnum flashed an embarrassed smile. He was still too happy about seeing his friends to take any comments like that the wrong way. "You didn't have to come looking for me."

"Yeah, but I'm not all that patient," Grinchard said. "And it's going to be dark soon."

"It's not like you to wander outside town this late in the day," Mycra said. "We worried that something might have gone wrong."

An awful feeling struck Farnum in the gut. "You didn't form a search party, did you?"

Mycra chucked him on the shoulder. "Don't worry yourself. It's just the two of us."

Grinchard rolled his eyes. "I told her that if we couldn't find you on our own there wasn't much chance anyone else would manage it either."

Grinchard's cavalier attitude toward his safety might have upset Farnum if he hadn't been so relieved. The entire town had come out to look for him when he'd gotten lost in the Underworld as a kid, and he was still living that horrible incident down. The last thing he wanted was to get the rest of the tongues around town wagging about that again.

Mycra craned her neck around, peering at the parts of the cave the torchlight reached. "Anyhow, now that we've found you, we should start working our way back home. If we head out now, we can get back to town before dark, and I'd rather not be roaming around at night."

Farnum gave Grinchard and Mycra a grateful nod. "You really are the best friends anyone could ever ask for."

"Remember that the next time we need something from you too!" Grinchard said with a cackle.

The irony was that Grinchard rarely needed anything from anyone. They didn't own a house. They usually slept out under the stars instead, or built a small shelter whenever they needed it. The only thing they owned that they treasured was their sword, and they made their living by its use, offering protection to those who needed it.

Grinchard often disappeared for weeks or even months at a time, but they always came back home eventually. Often they returned with little more than stories of their travels, but those were amazing enough that no one ever complained.

"I still don't understand how you found me," Farnum said as he side-eyed the entrance to the cave.

"I've gotten to be a pretty decent tracker," Grinchard said. "Which you'd know if you ever came out into the wild with me. And you left a trail as wide as a road."

"Is that a bad thing?"

Mycra smiled at him. "Not if you want to be found."

Farnum glanced back toward the cave mouth with a sigh. He'd spent so long trying to get up his courage to explore inside it that the moment had passed.

"Maybe you didn't want to?" Grinchard asked with a gleam of mischief in their eye. "You were eyeing that cave like you wanted to claim it!"

Mycra arched a disapproving eyebrow at Grinchard. "Have you forgotten the time Farnum got himself trapped underground when we were all kids? Stuck down below, surrounded by obsidian, unable to do anything to dig himself out?" She gave Farnum a concerned look. "How long were you down there again?"

"Two days," Farnum said as he fought off the memories that threatened to swallow him. "It was two days."

"I'm sure it seemed a lot longer," Mycra offered. "Imagine being stuck down there in that absolute blackness for so long. No way to mark the passing of time. No way to know if you'd ever escape it . . ."

Her voice trailed off in sympathy for Farnum's plight.

"I don't have to imagine it," he said. "I was there. You're right. It was awful."

Grinchard put their hand on the hilt of their sword and scoffed. "It was an awful long time ago."

That drew Farnum up short for a moment. "I still have nightmares about it." He noticed pity welling in Mycra's eyes, and he quickly added, "Not every night. You know. Just now and again."

"Ah, so that's why you never want to go exploring," Grinchard said.

"Or mining!" said Mycra, perhaps a bit too loudly. Farnum and Grinchard stared at her. "What? It's the best thing in the world! He doesn't know what he's missing out on!"

"You really ought to give it a try," Grinchard said to Farnum.

"Oh, don't give him a hard time about it." Mycra turned to Farnum to apologize. "I'm sorry about that. I get overexcited sometimes."

Then she turned back to Grinchard. "Do you not understand? Do you think he's such a homebody by nature? Why do you think he started a zoo rather than try his hand at something that might take him out of town?"

Grinchard shrugged. "You and I go off and have all sorts of wild adventures. We wander around all over the place. We have exciting jobs that people praise us for constantly. I did figure he's just a homebody. You know, like most people around here."

Farnum opened his mouth to protest, but Mycra interrupted him. "That's not fair!"

"If you say so." Grinchard clearly wasn't convinced. "He's been stuck here for years, working in a so-called zoo in which the most exotic attractions are things you can find on nearly any farm."

"Now, wait," Farnum said. "That may be true —"

"But it's all rooted in his childhood trauma," Mycra said, defending him. "That horrible incident that haunts him to this day! And you think he's just going to forget about that, reach deep down inside himself for some hidden scrap of bravery, and charge off into the unknown?"

"Now just a minute," Farnum spluttered, finally getting Mycra to stop. "Yes, maybe I was traumatized by that incident underground all those years ago. And yes, maybe it has made me afraid to venture out into the world like the rest of you. But that doesn't mean I'm a lost cause! Does it?"

Grinchard and Mycra suddenly found there were fascinating things to look at elsewhere, each of which just happened to be in the opposite direction of Farnum. It took Farnum a moment to realize that neither of them wanted to answer him, which disappointed him even more. "Well?" he demanded.

"Of course not," Mycra blurted out.

"That's not really up to us," Grinchard said carefully.

"Well, who's it up to then? I have a zoo to run. I can't just take off at the drop of a hat."

Grinchard frowned, uncomfortable with the topic but ready to forge ahead. "I saw you staring into that cave when we strolled up here. You nearly jumped out of your skin when we said hello."

Farnum flushed with embarrassment. "So?"

Grinchard shrugged. "So, maybe you should go in there."

The blood that had risen to Farnum's cheeks abruptly drained from them. "What now?"

"We're already here." Grinchard forced an easy smile. "No better time than the present, right?"

Farnum's mind cast around for some sort of excuse to get out of this. "I thought you said we had to head back. It's getting late in the day."

Grinchard chuckled. "Mycra said that. Not me."

Farnum turned to Mycra for help, and she sucked at her teeth as she peered up at the sky. "I was just trying to give you an easy way out of here. It's not that late. I mean, depending on how big the cave is and how far we want to go into it . . ."

Farnum went from disappointed to angry. "So if I don't charge off on some crazy expedition into the darkest and deepest parts of the world, I'm a lost cause then? Is that it? Forever? That hardly seems fair!"

Mycra gave him a sympathetic shrug. "That's not it. Not really. We love you either way, Farnum."

"I just came back here happy to see you," Grinchard said with a smile that asked Farnum to forget all about this.

Farnum considered letting his anger get away with him and marching off on his own right then and there. He appreciated them coming to find him, but he hated it when people treated him like this—especially his friends.

He could have just yelled at them and demanded that they leave him alone. They'd leave and wander back to town, and he might never speak to them again. Worse yet, if he did speak to them again, would they still be friends?

He glared at both of them in turn, and he didn't see the judgment he feared he might find in their eyes. All he saw there was genuine concern.

They really did care about him. If he didn't go with them, he knew they'd forgive him for it.

But would he ever be able to forgive himself?

He pursed his lips as if they were wrestling with each other before he finally opened his mouth to speak.

"All right," he said with a deep sigh. They might have been the hardest words he'd ever uttered. He knew once they left his lips there would be no turning back.

"All right?" Grinchard said, confused, unsure if Farnum had decided to end their friendship or not. "All right what?"

Farnum cringed just a bit. Making the decision had been hard enough. Now they were going to make him explain it to them? "All right, let's go." He waited for realization to dawn on them, but they were taking too long. "I'm in!"

"You're in?" Grinchard said in disbelief.

"You're in," Mycra said in awe.

"I'm in." Part of Farnum was relieved to finally be doing something like this with his friends. Finally facing up to his long-held fears. Finally doing something he was afraid of for once.

The other part of him wondered what in the world he'd gotten himself into.

HEADING IN

Farnum wasn't sure if his friends were just humoring him or not, but the idea that they were taking him seriously about going into the cave gave him a bit of a thrill. They'd all seen so much more of the world than he had that he felt ashamed sometimes, but maybe this would be the first step toward rectifying that.

It also terrified him, but he was trying to ignore that. He had already stood outside of this cave for much longer than he cared to admit, trying to force himself to enter it. With his friends at his side, he felt confident he could finally do it.

Grinchard reached into their own backpack, produced a torch, and lit it. Mycra did the same, shooting Farnum a questioning glance as she did. He just stared at her, clueless as to what she meant by it.

"Do you have a torch?" she finally said.

"Oh!" He did, and he fished it out of his pack as fast as he could. He fumbled a bit trying to light it, but he got it going fast enough and then held it up in front of himself in triumph.

As he did, he saw that the others were long since ready to move. They glanced at each other, and Grinchard gave Mycra a firm nod. "I'll lead the way."

Farnum opened his mouth to protest, but Grinchard was already striding into the cave, their torch held high before them.

Farnum hesitated only a moment before following Grinchard in. He stopped once he was inside the cave to peer at how their flickering lights pushed back the darkness and to see what they might reveal.

One of the reasons that Farnum hadn't been able to enter before—among many—was that he worried that some dangerous mob might have set up residence in the cave, turning it into its lair. He supposed he should have been excited about the possibility of finding a strange new mob that he might be able to bring back to his zoo, but the fear of being eaten did a fine job of tempering that.

"Keep your eyes peeled for mobs," he called out to Grinchard. "Both good ones and bad ones."

"There's a difference?"

"The good ones don't try to kill you."

Grinchard laughed, entirely unworried. "But the 'bad ones' would make fantastic additions to your zoo!"

The explorer had a point. Dangerous mobs could certainly get people more interested in visiting his zoo. He just didn't know if he wanted to try to take care of such beasts. Sure, it would mean more money, but would it be worth the risk?

A part of him thought that all creatures deserved to be cared for, but even he had a hard time arguing that was true for things like zombies and creepers. The chance to study them up close, though, was tempting.

In any case, the cave seemed to be abandoned. No mobs were living in it—at least as far as the torchlight could reveal.

This both relieved Farnum and disappointed him.

"It's empty," he said.

Mycra came up behind him and gestured deeper into the cave with her torch. "So go on in."

Farnum swallowed hard and did just that. It turned out to be much easier than his fears had told him it would be. Grinchard went before them, lighting the way and proving there was nothing to be scared about.

"See?" the explorer said with a wide grin. "Nothing to it."

Farnum had to admit to himself that his friends had been right. He'd been letting his trepidation take control and keep him from exploring the wider world that he'd always wanted to explore. While he was still terrified of the cave, having them here with him made all the difference.

They wandered through the entire cave from one end to the other, and nothing jumped out to eat them at all. In fact, as far as Farnum could tell, the three of them were the only living creatures in the entire place.

Despite himself, he heaved a deep sigh of relief, letting out a breath he hadn't realized he was holding.

The only thing they did spot in the cave were some plants in one of the far corners. Grinchard identified them immediately. "Hey, look! Azalea!"

"That's lucky," Grinchard said. "You don't see these everywhere, you know."

"What's so lucky about it?" Farnum genuinely wanted to know.

"Azalea roots often grow from one cave down into another. If we follow them, we might find a whole other cave below them."

Farnum felt his heart skip a beat as he considered the prospect of digging into what he called the Underworld and moving even farther away from the mouth of the cave they were already in. "And that's a good thing?"

"It is if you like exploring." Grinchard clapped him on the back. "We didn't find any animals for your zoo here, but it's probably not that far down to the next cave. It can't hurt to look."

"Are you sure about that?" Farnum could think of lots of ways that it could hurt, right off the top of his head.

Grinchard chuckled. "Can you ever really be sure about anything?"

Mycra saw the look on Farnum's face and came over to reassure him. "They're right about the azalea. Their roots often lead straight down to another cave, one that's been protected from the surface by being sealed in. It's amazing what you can sometimes find down there: metals, minerals, even creatures."

Farnum knew that she'd tossed that last one in just to hook him. He also knew that it had worked.

"You've already come this far," she said softly.

He gave her a reluctant nod. "I suppose it can't hurt to look . . ."

Mycra grinned at him as she bounced with excitement. "May I do the honors?" She pulled out a diamond shovel. As a professional miner, she relied on her tools, and she'd invested in making sure she had the best.

Grinchard chuckled as they waved her toward the plant. "Be my guest."

Farnum took a deep breath. He knew that Mycra didn't really need such a fancy tool to follow the roots of an azalea, but the fact that she was using professional equipment like that suddenly made it all seem much more real.

Like she was really digging a mine shaft.

And he was going to follow her into it.

He wasn't sure that he'd have been able to do such a thing on his own. Actually, he was positive he would have balked at it. The idea of digging his own way through the Underworld still scared him. But he thought at least that maybe he could follow his professional friend—who had tons of experience and knew what she was doing and would never, ever abandon him—into a tunnel she was digging.

Mycra led the way, then Farnum, with Grinchard bringing up the rear. She dug straight into the rooted dirt below them, following the path of the azalea's roots. With a little nudge from Grinchard, Farnum kept up right behind her, giving her just enough room to swing her shovel without smacking him with it.

Whether the others had intended it or not, their marching orders helped Farnum feel safe. With one friend ahead and another behind, he seemed protected from anything horrible that could happen to him. The Underworld might fill him with all sorts of worries, but his friends helped him push those worries aside.

As Mycra worked, Farnum admitted to himself that he wished he'd tried doing this with them before—a long time ago. He'd wasted so much time being held back by his fears.

But he was here now, at least, having the adventure of his life.

He couldn't help but smile, even though no one else could see it.

He was still smiling when Mycra's shovel broke into a new cave below them. As expert at mining as she was, she didn't fall through the roof of that cave like Farnum probably would have. Instead, she called a quick halt while she stuffed a lit torch through the hole she'd dug and peered into the cavern beyond.

"It's pretty big," she reported back a moment later. "It goes on much farther than I can see."

Farnum couldn't help asking a nervous question. "How are we going to get to the cavern's floor from all the way up here?"

Mycra gave him an understanding laugh. "We got lucky. It's not that far down from here. Just a short drop. Should be easy enough." She saw the doubt in Farnum's eyes and made him a quick offer to reassure him. "I'll go first!"

Without even waiting for a response from Farnum, much less anyone else, Mycra slipped down through the hole she'd carved out and disappeared. Farnum listened hard but didn't hear her hit the bottom. Frightened for his friend, he darted forward and stuck his head through the hole after her.

"Mycra!"

He heard a giggle, and a moment later Mycra lit a torch and looked up at him from where she'd landed on a bunch of azaleas clustered together beneath her like a bed. "Come on down!" she called up to him. "It's fine!"

Farnum fell back and took a moment to steel himself. For a horrible moment, he worried that Grinchard might push past him and leave him alone in the tunnel. When he glanced back, though, he saw his friend patiently gesturing for him to proceed down the hole.

"When you're ready," Grinchard said.

With a little nod to Grinchard, Farnum lowered himself slowly through the hole until his arms couldn't stretch any longer. He thought he was only a few feet above the cave's floor, but he still hung there for a moment, waiting for his fingers to get tired, before he let go and landed on the soft plants below.

As he landed, the impact let him expel a huge breath, and he began to laugh quietly at himself. A moment later, Grinchard landed right next to him and patted him on the back.

"Just look at it," Mycra said breathlessly. "It's beautiful!"

Farnum stopped chuckling and did as Mycra requested. Instantly, awe overtook him as well.

The cave was huge, much larger than the one they'd just been in. The walls and ceiling were covered with hanging vines laced with more glow berries than he'd ever seen in his entire life up to that point. They lit up the place like a moon that had been smashed to smithereens and was shining from inside the cavern's walls.

Besides the patch of azalea they'd landed in, other stands of it appeared along the uneven floor as it undulated beneath the arched ceiling. They would have plenty of choices for roots to follow from there if they wanted to. Maybe too many.

Farnum turned to the others to apologize to them for dragging his feet about coming here. He felt bad about making so many excuses for not leaving town before. He should have gone with them on an adventure long before this.

But they weren't paying any attention to him and apparently didn't share his worries. Mycra was too busy gawking at everything around them to worry about Farnum and how he'd finally managed to overcome his long-standing fears. He didn't have the heart to interrupt her right then.

Instead Farnum turned to Grinchard and discovered that his friend had a huge smile on their face. The explorer waved their hand to indicate the whole scene around them and how amazing it was. "What did I tell you?"

KEEP GOING

"I know." Farnum shook his head at himself. "I should have done something like this a long time ago, right?"

"You're absolutely right about that." Grinchard just kept grinning at him.

Farnum stared at their surroundings. The cave seemed to go on forever. "So, is this the biggest cave you've ever been in?"

Grinchard snickered at the thought. "Not even close. There's one a ways south of here that's at least ten times as big as this one, if you can believe that." They stretched their arms as wide as they could make them. "*Much* bigger."

"Then why are you smiling like that?"

Grinchard ran their tongue across their teeth and smiled even wider. "Because it's still amazing, isn't it?"

Farnum could only nod and agree.

"And on top of that, I get to share it with my two best friends. What could be better?"

With that, Grinchard charged off into the cavern, their torch pushing back the dimness as they went. They cackled the entire way.

"What are they doing?" Farnum said, shaking his head. "Are they okay?"

Mycra laughed at him. "Exploring! And loving it!"

She shot Farnum a mischievous look and then a *what are you gonna do* shrug. Then she went racing after Grinchard before veering off in a direction of her own, giggling as she went.

Farnum hesitated for just the briefest of moments and then started after his friends. At about the point where Mycra's path had diverged from Grinchard's, he sailed off in a direction entirely his own.

Farnum was so caught up in the moment that it didn't even occur to him to be scared. This place was just too amazing, and he could hear his friends' laughs echoing off the walls all around him. It felt like they were with him every step of the way.

Not too far along, he came upon an underground river burbling right through the middle of the cavern. Perhaps the water was what had carved the place out of the mountain in the first place, he thought. He wondered where it had come from, and then he wondered where it might take him.

Feeling free, he followed the current and the wandering edges of the river, letting it guide his way through the cave. That's when he spotted them.

The axolotls.

He'd read about these amphibious creatures before and studied pictures of them in books, but he'd never come close to seeing one in real life. The moment he saw them, though, he immediately knew what they had to be.

They were small creatures with damp skin, thick bodies, and

long spindly limbs. They had wide eyes that looked like they could see straight through you, and their wide mouths seemed like they were constantly smiling at you.

He was smitten with them straightaway, and he knew right then that he had to bring at least one of them back to show at his zoo. He reached into his pack and pulled out one of the water buckets that he always carried with him for just such an occasion. He hadn't had much opportunity to use it over the years, and he sometimes wondered why he still bothered with it. Some sense of obstinance or destiny had kept it there in his pack for the moment he needed it: right now.

All those doubts vanished as he charged toward the axolotls, the bucket raised high over his head. As he reached the group of axolotls, he brought the bucket down, and to his great astonishment he snagged one of the slippery creatures with it!

He brought the bucket up before him and gawked at the wriggling creature trapped inside it, his eyes even wider than its own. It stared back at him, unsure of what to make of the person who had snatched it up out of the river's chilly waters, and he instantly felt attached to it and started to comfort it.

"It's all right, little fella," he said to it in soothing tones. "Everything's going to be fine. I'm not going to hurt you. In fact, I'm going to bring you home to my zoo and keep you well fed and safe!"

The axolotl kept wriggling for a bit, more than a little suspicious of Farnum and his bucket, but it eventually surrendered to the moment and decided to ride along and see where the strange person took him.

"Woo-hoo!" Farnum shouted, startling the axolotl into wriggling around the inside of the bucket again.

"Are you okay?" Mycra called back. Her voice echoed off the cavern's walls so hard it was impossible to tell in which direction she stood.

"Never better!" Farnum responded. "This place is amazing!"

"I told you so!" Grinchard shouted from an entirely different direction—or so it seemed. Farnum couldn't say for sure.

"Where are the two of you anyhow?" Mycra called, curious. "This place is incredible, but maybe we shouldn't lose one another in it!"

Grinchard let loose a big belly laugh. "Live a little! Go explore for a bit! When we're done, we can meet back by the way we came in!"

That sounded fantastic to Farnum. He was glad that Mycra had expressed some worry about it before he had, though. He didn't like to be the spoilsport every time, and he was having far too much fun at the moment to give voice to such concerns.

He looked at the axolotl swinging in his bucket, and he grinned at it. Just think about how excited folks back in town would be to see such a creature. It would be the highlight of the zoo!

Then something else in the river caught his eye. At first he wasn't quite sure what it could be. It was just a flash of white against the midnight blue of the river, but that was enough to pique his curiosity. He had to get closer.

Carrying the captured axolotl before him, Farnum moved farther down the river, searching for another sign of what he'd seen—or at least thought he had. At first it eluded him, and he only saw the surface of the river, its swift currents sending ripples undulating along it.

Then he saw it again, sharper this time. Something almost a glowing white breached the surface, poked its head up, and then submerged again.

The sight of it stopped Farnum's breath in his chest. He knew instantly both what it had to be and that it was, at the same time, utterly impossible.

A leucistic axolotl.

Living in caves, far from the light of the sun, caused some creatures to lose all of the pigmentation—the color—in their skin. This turned them a ghostly white, the exact color Farnum had seen moving in the water.

Most axolotls came in pretty definite colors. Finding a leucistic one with such luminous skin was incredibly rare—or so his mobology books told him. To think that he might be within reach of one sent his heart fluttering.

Realizing that he'd stopped breathing, Farnum drew in one large gasp of disbelief. Then he started moving toward the stunning creature he'd seen, hoping that he could spot it again.

As he moved, he pulled out another water bucket. He wasn't sure how he would be able to carry two axolotls back to the surface with him, but that was a problem he could solve later.

Maybe Mycra would carry the one he'd already caught. If Farnum managed to capture a leucistic axolotl, he was sure he would never want to put it down until it was safe and sound in his zoo.

But he had to catch it first.

When he reached the place where he'd seen the creature swimming, it was gone. He supposed that was to be expected. It looked like it had been moving deeper into the water, and the current would have carried it along. He had to search for it farther downstream.

He squinted hard and stared at the river until it seemed to be staring back at him, but he couldn't see anything but the reflection of his torchlight on the water. He realized he'd have a better shot at seeing the rare axolotl's skin without the light than with it, so he put the torch out.

His eyes adjusted quickly to the dimness, still illuminated softly by the glow berries hanging throughout the vines that festooned the place. They helped, but it still wasn't quite enough.

He decided to enter the river itself to get a better angle. The water was cold and clear, running over rocks instead of mud, and he found he could see through it as if it were glass.

The reflection of the glow berries still made it hard to see things farther away from him, though. He decided to try one more thing. He took a deep breath and plunged entirely under the water's surface.

The icy waters nearly shocked the air out of Farnum's lungs, but he managed to steady himself. He let his watertight pack float on the surface above him, which made it easier for him to hold his already-filled bucket up out of the water.

Farnum peered through the icy water, looking farther downstream than he'd been able to manage before, and he spotted it! There it was, clear as day: the leucistic axolotl!

The pale creature didn't seem to notice Farnum at all. There probably weren't many predators down here that it would need to keep its guard up against, so it likely wouldn't pay much attention to Farnum, even if it saw him.

Farnum decided to use that to his advantage. He surfaced just long enough to grab a fresh breath of air, then plunged back down into the water and began swimming toward the creature, entirely submerged.

The entire time, the pale creature seemed to be getting closer and closer, making Farnum more and more determined to catch up with it. What a find it would be!

But then it disappeared altogether in less than an instant. Confused, Farnum pushed forward, swimming faster, hoping that the creature had simply rounded a bend in the river.

In a way, it had.

Farnum was too preoccupied with wondering if the river bent left or right at that point to consider the other option. He darted forward as fast as he could, determined not to let the leucistic axolotl get away.

That's why he didn't see the waterfall until he was staring right over it.

RESCUE YOURSELF

Before Farnum knew what was happening, the river's current grew more powerful than he could imagine. It felt like a giant had grabbed him and was pulling him along now. He turned around and tried to swim in the other direction, but it did him no good.

He was so desperate at this point that he even let go of the bucket in which he was carrying the axolotl he'd already captured. As precious as having that creature was to him—as much as it could mean to his zoo—it wasn't going to be any help to him if he never made it back home alive.

Farnum tried swimming against the current with all his might, but the current only got stronger at that point and pulled him along faster. Terrified, he struggled to the surface and gasped for air. As he did, he turned about and saw that the ceiling of the cave was coming right down on top of him. Soon there wouldn't be a surface to return to.

"Help!" he shouted at the top of his lungs. "Help me!"

That was all he managed to get out before the current swept him beneath the surface again, and he knew it would do him no good. The echoes in the cave would keep his friends from figuring out even which way he'd gone.

And it was already far too late.

Despite his utter panic, Farnum decided that the only thing to do was to go with the current. In fact, he turned to swim *with* it. He only had so much air left inside him, and he wasn't going to waste it trying to fight the current.

His last hope was that the river would wind up in another cave again fast. Otherwise he would drown for sure.

He had just turned around when the bottom of the river dropped out entirely and took him with it. If he could have, he would have screamed the whole way down.

He could only tell he'd hit the bottom of the waterfall by the way his descent slowed almost to a stop. At that point, the water above him began pounding down on him mercilessly, keeping him pinned down.

Exhausted, he realized that he couldn't fight such power. The only thing he could do was go with the flow.

He let the current push him down hard enough that he bounced off the rocks below. The impact scraped and bruised him, but it also knocked him out of the center of the waterfall, pushing him out and away from its base.

A moment later, Farnum popped up out of the river like a fishing bobber. As he breached the surface, he instinctively gasped for air, and he felt like he'd never tasted anything so amazing. The blackness that had been rising in around the edges of his vision retreated, and he saw that he was in another cave.

This one had a high ceiling covered with vines and glow berries, much like the one he'd just left, but it wasn't nearly as lush, at least in the parts of it that he could see. The river widened here, and its current slowed to a crawl.

After floating along with the flow for a moment—just long enough to catch his breath and let his heartbeat return to normal—Farnum reached down with his feet and realized he could touch the ground. Better than that, he could actually stand.

With his feet finally beneath him, Farnum stretched up to his full height and discovered the river was only waist-high here. He stood against the current and surveyed this new cave.

It seemed that the river covered most of the cave's floor. If it hadn't been for its high ceiling, Farnum likely would have drowned. By the light of the glow berries, he could only see a single patch of dry land, off to the river's left.

He decided to make for it, being careful to watch for sinkholes or other hazards in the water. While he was at it, he kept an eye out for the leucistic axolotl, but he didn't see it anywhere.

His heart sank at that. He'd gone through so much and was honestly happy just to be alive at this point, but finding that pale amphibian might have made the ordeal feel at least a little bit worth it.

As he made it to the little island on the river's edge, though, he spotted the axolotl he'd captured before. It was still in his bucket, but despite that it seemed no worse for the wear. It alternately swam about in the bucket's depths and then stretched out on the water's surface as if sunning itself on a riverbank.

Farnum sat down next to the captured axolotl and reached out a hand to pet it. To his delight, it brought its head up to meet his hand.

While he didn't want to lose the creature, he decided that it didn't make much sense for him to keep it in the bucket if they had no way out of the cave anyhow. If something happened to him, he didn't want the axolotl to be trapped too. He tipped over the bucket and let the creature out.

The axolotl stared up at him for a moment. Then it padded over to him and raised its head to him for more petting. Farnum was delighted to oblige him.

"Don't worry," he said to the axolotl. "I'll get us out of here soon."

He gazed out at their surroundings. "I'm just not sure how."

Satisfied with the petting, the axolotl turned around and began to explore their new surroundings on its own. Tired and not quite ready to face their predicament, Farnum watched the creature wander off. It crawled its way across the small island toward the far end of it.

Something just beyond the axolotl caught Farnum's eye. At first, he wasn't sure what it was. It just seemed like a blackness in the darkness, but it was sharp, tall, and rectangular, shaped something like a door.

But what would a door be doing down here?

Curious, Farnum pushed himself to his feet and staggered over toward the dark rectangle. As he got closer, he realized it was just the frame of a gateway standing there on the edge of the island, with no walls around it. Not only did it not touch the cave's wall, it didn't have anything inside of it.

He didn't understand why someone would have put such a thing there, or what use it might have had. Was it simply a piece of art? Had there been a building of some sort there once?

The gateway—if that's what it was—seemed to have been fashioned entirely of a black volcanic rock. That was mysterious enough, but as Farnum gazed through it, he saw something that he understood even less.

The cavern wall behind the gateway was covered with some kind of writing that formed a gigantic story as massive as a mural. He couldn't read any of it, and he wasn't even sure if the symbols he saw on the wall were letters. He stared closely at them and realized that many of them looked more like crude pictures instead.

He'd never seen anything like it, and despite the fact he was trapped deep in the Underworld and had lost track of his friends as well, he wanted to take a closer look at it. The light from the glow berries, though, wasn't enough. He needed something better.

That's when Farnum's stomach growled and reminded him there were other concerns in a person's life than just light. The fact that he was also still shivering from being wet made him realize there was something he could build that would solve a number of his problems at once.

Farnum reached into his pack and pulled out some logs, some sticks, and a lump of coal and assembled them in a neat pile for a fire. Upon inspection, they all seemed like they'd stayed dry enough in his pack, even though he'd gone over a waterfall with them. He decided not to question his luck.

He reached even deeper into the pack and pulled out his flint and steel. He wasn't as experienced at using such things as his friends, but he knew how they worked. He just needed to strike them together enough to produce a spark that could ignite the campfire. Simple, right?

He tried it a few times, but nothing happened. The flint and steel produced sparks, but they didn't catch with the firewood.

He decided he needed both hands to work the flint and steel

so he could really get some sparks going. He knelt down next to that odd frame and struck the flint and steel again and again and again.

Soon enough he had a roaring campfire going, and the heat and light it threw off made the cave seem much cozier. He lit a torch with it and gazed up at the pictures on the wall to get a better look at them, but they still didn't make much sense.

He set the torch down next to the odd frame and was about to dig into his pack to find something to cook for a meal. That's when he noticed that the gateway had filled in with a deep purpling swirl that had started to glow.

HELLO

"You have failed me for the last time, Kritten!" The Great Bungus stormed off the blackstone chair they liked to refer to as their throne and drew their golden axe, brandishing it before themself. "No more words! All that's left for you is doom!

Kritten cringed away, retreating toward the back of the room. It seemed unlikely that Bungus would actually smack down one of their most important advisors on the spot, but the piglin ruler had done stranger things before. Keeping their temper in check was not one of Bungus's strongest traits.

"I did everything you asked! I tried everything I could think of! It's no use!"

"Then we have no use for you! Get out of here, and don't ever come back!"

Kritten blanched at the prospect of being booted from the bastion and having to make their way through the Nether on their own. "You should just squash me now! It would be faster and less miserable than wandering the wastes all alone!"

Bungus moved toward Kritten, keeping the axe between them and forcing them into a corner. As Bungus drew closer, Kritten eyed the guards at the exit, looking for a means of escape.

They weren't looking at Bungus and Kritten at all. In fact, they were taking great pains not to look at them for fear of the Great Bungus's anger becoming focused on them instead.

"Come here then!" Bungus said. "I can help you get rid of that living problem you have right now!"

Under normal circumstances, Kritten might have just stayed in this room with Bungus and taken their lumps, but the look in Bungus's eyes was absolutely furious. If Kritten wanted to get through this, they needed to leave—now.

Kritten did the one thing that Bungus wasn't expecting at all. They charged straight at him and kicked the big brute in the knee.

Bungus dropped their golden axe to clutch at their kneecap and howl in pain. The guards rushed in from the doorway to see what was happening. When they saw Bungus curled up on the floor and yowling, they rushed to the leader's side to see if they could help.

Kritten took advantage of that moment to flee. An instant later, they were through the doorway and into the bastion proper, looking for somewhere to hide.

A shout of alarm went up in the throne room, though, which meant that nowhere in the entire complex would be safe. If they found Kritten, the best the advisor could hope for was to be thrown out into the Nether from something not quite as high as the bastion's tallest tower.

As much as it pained Kritten to admit it, the best choice for their future would be to leave the bastion via the front door, under their own power. Being banished into the Nether to survive all alone would be bad enough, but trying to do so with broken legs would be impossible.

Kritten skulked through the halls of the bastion, stealing everything they could find that they thought might help them once they were on their own. Food for sure. A bit of warped fungus, which could be used to keep any roaming hoglins away. Some Nether wart, which had so many uses, especially for a piglin as smart as Kritten. A heavy sack full of gold. And a golden axe that they pilfered from Uggub's private quarters.

Not that they knew how to use one well.

Kritten had managed to rise so high among the piglins by being smart. Most piglins seemed—to Kritten, at least—to care only about power. They liked to bully one another by means of raw strength and viciousness, and the biggest bully of them all got to be in charge—at least until a bigger bully came along.

Brute force mattered to them more than anything else, but not to Kritten. The advisor was short and small and not all that good with even the most popular piglin weapon: the crossbow. All of those things combined definitely ruled out Kritten using muscle to get their way. The only thing left to them had been their brains, and they'd taken great pains to study hard and test them well to keep them sharper than any blade.

Till today, that had seemed like a wonderful strategy.

Since Kritten couldn't boss around other piglins by force of their arms, they had opted to find and back a gigantic piglin instead. Before Kritten had found Bungus, the brute had not had any ambitions beyond beating up other piglins and taking their food. With Kritten's guidance, though, Bungus had gone from simple bully to the ruler of an entire bastion and all of the piglins in it.

For a long time, Bungus had been grateful to Kritten for all the help. The brute knew that they never would have gotten so far without having such a clever advisor behind them. But now that they had reached the top of the piglin heap, the responsibilities of leadership had started to outweigh the benefits, and Bungus's gratitude had faded fast.

Bungus's thankfulness had morphed into suspicion and now transformed into outright hostility.

Kritten didn't blame Bungus for this. Instead, they took the blame for doing such a poor job of imagining how this could happen. They should have predicted it and worked out a way to stop it from happening—or for replacing Bungus before it got to this point.

That wasn't entirely true, though. There was one other piglin whom Kritten held responsible for Bungus's awful change in attitude: Uggub.

As Bungus's second-in-command, Uggub had always been pouring poison about Kritten into the leader's ear. They clearly wanted to get rid of Bungus and take over ruling the bastion instead, but Kritten had always stood in the way of that. While driving Bungus to fits with warnings and complaints, Uggub had steered the blame for these issues straight to Kritten, even if Kritten was actually entirely blameless.

Unfortunately, Kritten hadn't figured that out in time to stop it from happening. Now Kritten wondered if maybe Uggub wasn't a lot smarter than they appeared. Maybe not in terms of book learning or research, but certainly with regard to base piglin cunning.

Kritten was going to have to rethink their own strategy for how to deal with such things—if they managed to survive this.

Having gathered everything they could manage to carry if

not everything they might actually need, Kritten made their way for the bastion's front doors. Bungus's bellowing still echoed through the halls, and everyone that Kritten saw just pressed right past them on their way to the throne room to see what all the commotion could possibly be about. No one tried to stop them at all.

At least not until they actually reached the gates.

Uggub stood there waiting for them, arms crossed in front of them. The massive piglin blocked the way out entirely, and when they saw Kritten they sneered at them and asked, "Where do you think you're going?"

"I'm just following orders!" Kritten lied, happy that they'd tucked Uggub's axe away in their pack. "I wasn't able to solve every last problem for the Great and Powerful Bungus, so I've been banished from the bastion!"

Uggub looked Kritten up and down, checking out all of the things they were carrying with them. "And Bungus gave you all that gear as a parting gift?"

Kritten snorted at Uggub for being stupid and implied that the Great Bungus had done exactly that: given the advisor all these things as a way to get rid of them. "You think it's so simple to just get rid of me? Like I don't know all sorts of secrets that the Great Bungus would rather not get out? Our great ruler might hate me right now, but that doesn't mean that they don't have to respect me!"

Uggub raised their eyebrows at that, reluctantly impressed. "I didn't think you had that in you!"

"I'm full of all sorts of surprises!"

Kritten pushed past Uggub, and the brute actually stood aside. Kritten wasn't sure if that was out of fear or respect or just simple relief that they had finally triumphed over their greatest rival for Bungus's attention and influence.

Either way, Uggub got out of the way and let Kritten pass. The advisor strode out of the bastion like they owned the place and would one day be back to reclaim it from the piglins that were holding it for them.

And then someone who actually knew the truth about how Kritten had left the Great Bungus's presence called out from the ramparts at the top of the bastion. "Is that Kritten? Stop them! The Great Bungus wants them dead!"

Kritten didn't even bother to glance back to see the look on Uggub's face. They just started running like they were never going to stop.

ON THE RUN

As Kritten sprinted away from the bastion, arrows arced out from the ramparts and fell all around them. Whether by intention or luck, not one of them hit the advisor, although one of them came close enough to poke a hole in their pack.

Kritten didn't try to dodge the arrows, which would have been next to impossible for them anyhow. They just kept their head down and their nose pointed forward and ran as fast as their little legs would take them.

Not for the first time in their life, Kritten wished they were bigger. Being smart was wonderful, but they would have been willing to trade a bit of their brains for longer, faster legs at that moment.

The fact that Kritten was outside the bastion and alone in the Nether would normally have terrified them, but being inside the bastion with all of the other piglins would have been much worse. It wasn't until they were well out of bowshot from the bastion that it even occurred to them that they should be afraid.

Kritten needed to find some kind of shelter as fast as they could, and not just a place to hide from Bungus's underlings. There were so many mobs in the Nether that would try to kill them on sight that the best defense against them was not to be seen in the first place.

The Great Bungus's bastion—well, the one that they had commandeered with Kritten's help—was one of the best bastions in the area. It was situated in a crimson forest, which offered it more protection than the open plains of the Nether wastes could ever have managed. The towering, blood-red fungi that made up the bulk of the forest gave Kritten lots of places to hide from arrows, and the soft glow of the shroomlights high up in the fungi made it easy to navigate through the dark red fog that pervaded the place. The only trick was to make sure that nothing was hiding behind those gigantic fungi to pounce out at them too.

Fortunately, Kritten had taken the time to scout out the area around the bastion long before this. Back then the idea had been to figure out what kinds of threats might reside close to the bastion so that the piglins could figure out how to get rid of them. In the back of their mind, though, Kritten had also been plotting out possible ways to escape from the bastion should everything there go bad.

To their shame, Kritten had honestly not thought that the Great Bungus would ever turn against them. After all, Kritten had engineered Bungus's rise to power. The leader depended on an advisor like Kritten and would be entirely lost without them.

In the end, though, Bungus hadn't seen it that way, had they?

Perhaps Kritten had let their ego get in their way. They'd gotten too comfortable in their chambers in the bastion—too used to life on top of the piglin heap. They'd spent so much time watching for threats from outside the bastion that they'd not bothered looking for threats from within.

At least Kritten had spotted a good hiding place all those months ago, a place that was both out of sight of the bastion and offered at least a little protection from other, non-piglin threats. Now all they needed to do was reach it.

Doing that didn't turn out to be too hard. The commotion at the bastion had attracted the attention of most of the other mobs in the area, and they had come to mill around the place to see what was happening. From long practice, they stayed just out of bowshot of the ramparts, but that didn't stop the piglins stationed there from trying their luck with a few arrows anyhow.

That worked in Kritten's favor, as it kept the attention of those mobs on the bastion while the advisor scrambled to find their hiding spot, hoping that it was still there. When they found it— a hole in the ground surrounded and hidden by a large square of giant fungus stumps—they dove into it and did not sigh with relief until they made sure that nothing else had decided to claim it as their den in the meantime.

It wasn't until then that Kritten unclenched enough to feel their heart trying to beat through their chest. They'd been in too much of a panic to worry about anything but imminent death till just now. The effort of keeping their head together that whole time had been exhausting, and they closed their eyes for what they told themselves would only be a short moment.

While they rested nestled in their stolen gear, Kritten started to plan out what their next steps might be. They couldn't just move into this little cave and live there. Eventually they'd run out of food and water, and they'd be forced out into the open. When that happened, they would be better off if they had a place to go.

There were other piglins out there in the Nether, Kritten knew. Some of them had bastions too, ones that hadn't been entirely destroyed by the mightiest of the roving mobs. Maybe Kritten could find one of them and ask them to take them in.

Most of the piglins in the area—especially the leaders—knew of Kritten as the Great Bungus's advisor. Kritten wondered if they'd be able to trade on that for a bit of kindness from those piglins.

The advisor grunted at the idea of other piglins being kind. They wouldn't do it out of the nonexistent goodness of their hearts. Kritten would have to offer them something in return, something of value. A lot of value. Like an entire hill's worth of gold—which they would then just steal from them.

The nearest clan seemed fond of tossing up poorly built structures—and then watching them fall down. Maybe Kritten could help them keep those places standing, but the advisor wasn't sure the clan would appreciate that.

The next closest clan had taken such a shine to the crimson forest's gigantic fungi that they almost seemed to worship them. Unfortunately, part of that worship involved never cleaning themselves, and Kritten's nose was too sensitive to tolerate that.

Another clan roamed through the region, riding hoglins through the forests from place to place like nomads. The real trick would be finding them, and even then Kritten had grown used to having a real roof overhead.

Piglins were greedy creatures, but the moment they saw Kritten they would know exactly how desperate the advisor had to be. The things Kritten had swiped on their way out of the Great Bungus's bastion wouldn't be enough. The gold Kritten was carrying might get them an audience to plead their case, but it would be too little to buy them a home.

They would have to offer that prospective piglin leader something more.

Something like the Great Bungus!

Kritten knew Bungus backward and forward: their strengths, their weaknesses, and every last bit about their bastion. If some ambitious piglin leader wanted to attack the bastion with an eye toward taking it from Bungus, the information Kritten could offer them would be invaluable. Instead of offering a sack of gold, Kritten would be able to provide them with all of Bungus's gold. Every bit of it.

In fact, Kritten might be able to parley that information into becoming the attacker's advisor, which would mean being restored to a place of honor and power in Bungus's very bastion. Kritten could then return to the rightful place that they had earned through all their hard work and cunning. The only difference would be that there would be someone other than Bungus in charge.

And this time around, Kritten wouldn't make the same mistakes. They'd be on the lookout for treachery from within. They'd take steps to make sure that no one could take their position away from them ever again.

All they had to do was find the right piglin to make it happen.

They nodded off with that warm and comforting thought in their head.

They were awakened not much later by someone grabbing them by the front of their shirt and hauling them bodily out of their hiding hole.

The attacker threw them out over the boulders that had hidden the place from casual view, and the impact with the ground knocked the wind right out of Kritten. As they lay in the dirt, struggling to catch their breath, the attacker vaulted over those same boulders and landed right in front of them, looming over the advisor, their shadow blocking out the sky.

It was Uggub, and they were laughing.

The brute leaned down over Kritten and stabbed a thick finger into the advisor's chest. "You think you're so smart, don't you? Smarter than any other piglin! Smarter than the Great Bungus! Even smarter than me!"

"No, wait—!"

Uggub wasn't done talking. "Well, maybe you are! But you're stupid too! If you were smart, you would have run all the way away! Not stopped here!"

"Please!"

Kritten had more to say, but Uggub scooped them up in a brutal grasp and starting hauling them away while continuing to berate them. "If you were really smart, you wouldn't have left a trail that led me right here! And you wouldn't be so weak that I can just drag you back!"

Kritten didn't believe that Uggub was a tracker of any skill. In fact, the brute had a hard time figuring out how to get around the bastion on most days. It was enough of a shock that Uggub had even left the bastion to go after Kritten, much less the brute having actually found them.

"But how—?"

Uggub shook the rest of the words right out of Kritten's mouth and then turned the advisor upside down so that they could see what the brute had meant. With their head hovering right over the ground, the advisor couldn't help but see a long line of pieces of Nether wart dribbled into the dirt that ran right over the path they'd taken to their hideaway.

Kritten still didn't quite understand how the line had gotten there. What had betrayed them? They thought they'd taken measures to be careful. They certainly hadn't left such a trail behind them, right?

Then a bit of Nether wart tumbled out of Kritten's punctured pack and into their face, and the advisor realized what had happened.

The arrow that had pierced Kritten's pack when they were fleeing from the bastion had punctured the sack of Nether wart they'd swiped. Pieces of Nether wart had spilled out behind them as they raced away, leaving a trail behind them that even someone as thickheaded as Uggub could follow.

Kritten wanted to smack a hand into their forehead for not having noticed this before it was far too late, but they were too discombobulated to manage it. That only got worse once Uggub heard Kritten gasp at this revelation. Laughing out loud, the brute swung Kritten around behind them by their ankles and began dragging the advisor along that way instead, seeming to take extra care and delight in thumping Kritten's head over every rock, bump, and fallen log they could find in the crimson forest.

"What an idiot you are!" Uggub said. "The problem isn't that you're smart! Next to most of us piglins, you might be a genius! The funny part is that you think you're smarter than you actually are!"

The brute chortled at that, but Kritten couldn't summon up enough wind to respond due to the constant thumping of their skull against the ground. They could only listen to that awful laugh.

Eventually Uggub came to an abrupt stop. "This should do!"

"What's happening?" By this point, Kritten had been battered nearly senseless. "Where are we?"

This didn't look like the bastion or anywhere near it. Kritten had expected Uggub to drag them back in front of the Great Bungus to hear the leader pronounce their punishment. At this point,

Kritten wouldn't have been surprised if that meant execution. After all, if Bungus had only wanted Kritten banished from the bastion, the advisor's escape from the place had already taken care of that.

"I'm not giving you another chance to calm down Bungus and talk your way out of your punishment!" Uggub said. "You got away with that too many times! Not today!"

With that, Uggub hauled Kritten up over his head. From this vantage point, the advisor could see that they stood on the edge of a pit right there on the edge of the crimson forest where it began to give way to the sprawling horror of the Nether wastes. Darkness swallowed the unseen bottom of it, but it seemed deep enough that falling into it would be fatal—much less being thrown into it!

"Today this all ends!" Uggub said. "And so do you!"

"No!" Kritten shouted. "No, no, no!"

They kept shouting it all the way down.

FINDING THE PORTAL

Kritten had no idea how much later it was when they awakened. They only knew that it was dark where they were — which was unusual in the Nether, where most of the place was continually lit by the roasting glow of lava.

Kritten got up on their elbows and looked around. The last thing they remembered was sailing through the open air into a pit. That and Uggub's horrible guffaws echoing after them.

The most amazing thing was that Kritten was alive at all. They had entirely expected to die then and there, and the fact that this hadn't happened seemed like a miracle. They decided to take the time to take an inventory of their injuries and evaluate whether or not there was any chance that they might be able to crawl out of this pit — if that was where they still were — under their own power.

Kritten discovered a number of bumps and bruises on their body, including a nasty knot on the back of their skull. They had a number of cuts and scrapes as well, but to the advisor's relief their body seemed to be intact.

The most stunning thing Kritten found was the creature on which they had apparently landed. It must have broken their fall, and if that was the case, that incredible accident had probably saved Kritten's life.

On the other hand, it hadn't done the creature nearly as much good. Kritten rolled off it to see if it had survived as well and was surprised to discover that—whatever it was—it was still breathing.

Kritten gazed upward and saw the shape of a hole high above them. That must be the rim of the pit into which Uggub had hurled them. Not much light came down through it, which meant Kritten had to strain their eyes to see anything.

Fortunately, it turned out that Uggub hadn't stripped Kritten of their pack before tossing them into the pit. It had gone flying while they tumbled into the pit, but it lay on the ground only a few feet away.

Kritten crawled over to the pack and fished a lantern out of it, then lit it. By its illumination, they could see that they weren't in a pit so much as a cave, the walls of which were too far away to be seen. There wasn't anyone—or anything—else in the place with them, at least as far as they could tell. Just the creature they'd landed upon.

Kritten moved back over to the creature and saw that it was a strider. The piglins loved striders, if only because they were the only mobs in the Nether that didn't seem like they were out to kill everyone around them. Also, you could climb on top of them and ride them anywhere, even across the hottest lava. On top of that, striders often shed strings that the piglins could use to help build crossbows and other handy things.

Kritten didn't know how this particular strider had gotten down here in this pit, apparently all by itself. Maybe it had fallen in. Maybe Uggub had tossed it in there first to see how deep the pit was.

In any case, Kritten was grateful that it had been there—and perhaps a little sorry that their unceremonious tumble into the pit had injured it. They wondered how they might help the strider. Maybe they could somehow nurse it back to health.

But first they had to figure out a way out of the pit, or they would wind up dying there next to the strider anyhow.

Kritten stood up, feeling every ache and bruise on their body, and held their lantern high. The walls that they could see around them were tall and steep, and there didn't seem to be an easy way out. It looked like an awful place to starve to death.

Kritten walked toward one wall and decided to follow it into the darkness. As they went, they saw that the wall curled around to the left—which they noticed only because of a purplish glow that emanated from around the bend.

Not wanting to alert whoever might be on the other side of the bend, Kritten extinguished their lantern and waited for their eyes to adjust to the darkness. They hadn't imagined the glow. They could see it even more strongly now, and they crept toward it as quietly as they could manage.

As they drew closer, they heard something around the corner as well. Kritten couldn't make it out all that well, but it sounded like someone talking to themself.

Kritten peered around the bend in the wall and had to suppress a gasp of surprise that would have certainly given them away. The purple glow was emanating from an obsidian portal!

Kritten had seen such portals in the past, but they had never seen one actually functioning. They always stood empty, hollow inside, waiting for someone or something to activate them.

Some mobs—including a fair number of piglins—liked to hang around obsidian portals and hope that they might light up so they could attack whatever came through them, but Kritten had always been too busy with other duties to simply hope that something might happen at some point. Word was that an active portal led from the Nether to a whole new world that worked differently from the one that Kritten knew, but that had always seemed like a ridiculous fantasy.

But here now was one that was actually working! And someone was standing in front of it!

Kritten knew an opportunity when they saw it. Hard as it was to believe it, Uggub might have actually done them a favor by tossing them down here. And now the advisor meant to take advantage of it.

Were they an ex-advisor now? Perhaps from the Great Bungus's point of view, but Kritten hadn't given up on their choice of career just yet. They'd find someone else to take them in as an advisor—or maybe they'd set themself up to rule a whole bastion themself instead.

If they only knew how. Uggub was right. Kritten was pretty smart, but smarts weren't enough to put a piglin in charge of a bastion. Brute strength was usually a lot more helpful in that regard.

Kritten drew Uggub's stolen axe from their pack and crept up behind the lone figure as quietly as possible. The advisor's feet didn't make a single sound, and they held their breath as well. Their heart pounded so hard, though, that they were surprised the person standing there and staring at the swirling purple inside the obsidian portal couldn't hear it.

The person even had their back to them! Kritten could not believe their luck!

Just as the advisor got within reach of the person, though, they turned around and bared their teeth at them.

Kritten knew that they might not get another chance, so they struck. They leaped out and tackled the person to the ground.

Kritten had never been much of a fighter—especially not compared to brutes like Uggub or the Great Bungus—so they were shocked when their victim bowled over backward so easily. Going with their momentum, Kritten scrambled up the person's body and put the blade of their axe to the person's throat.

Maybe a great piglin warrior would have simply dispatched the person with a few quick chops and then looted their body, but Kritten had never really hurt someone else, much less killed them. They hesitated instead, and that's when they saw that the person they'd attacked wasn't a piglin at all.

It was an Overworlder.

WHAT A BARGAIN

The terrified Overworlder threw their hands up and made a pitiful noise that was perhaps the least threatening thing that Kritten had ever heard. They kept their axe at the creature's throat, though, just in case, and shouted, "Who are you? What are you doing here? Tell me now!"

The Overworlder whimpered and said something in its unintelligible tongue. As far as Kritten knew, no one had ever been able to talk with an Overworlder, but that didn't seem to stop this terrified person from trying.

Kritten hadn't spent much time with Overworlders before. All they knew about them was that they came in two kinds. The first were tremendously powerful people who rampaged across the Nether, taking whatever they wanted and beating up anyone who got in their way.

The piglins understood these Overworlders. If the piglins could be nearly as strong and amazing as such invaders, they would do the exact same things. If anything, the piglins were jealous, and that jealousy often sent them into a frothing rage.

The second kind of Overworlders were weaklings who somehow managed to stumble through a portal and find themselves quickly overwhelmed by the Nether's vicious mobs. Lots of times they never even saw a piglin before they met their end. This one beneath Kritten's blade was clearly of that second type.

Most of these weakling Overworlders didn't stick around long enough for anyone to get to know them. They either were beaten down within minutes or they fled.

Maybe it was because this particular Overworlder seemed so pathetic, or perhaps it was due to the fact that Kritten had feared for their own life not so long ago, but the Overworlder's plight moved them to pity it. More than pity, though, in the back of Kritten's head they wondered if the Overworlder might be able to help them get out of this pit. Rather than steeling themself to put an end to the person, Kritten crawled right off and over their chest and then spun around and backed off a few feet.

The advisor wasn't that trusting, though. They still brandished their axe before them. If the Overworlder was shamming and trying to trick them into lowering their guard, they would be sorely disappointed.

For their part, the Overworlder took a moment to try to recover their dignity—if they had actually had any in the first place. Once they seemed to have control over themself once again, they sat up with their hands up, showing Kritten that they intended them no harm. The advisor wasn't sure they believed them, but they were willing to give this situation a chance to see where it went.

The Overworlder backed up while still on their rump until they were well outside of the reach of Kritten's axe. Even at that point, they made a huge show of being harmless and asking permission to stand. Feeling magnanimous—and perhaps a little more intimidating than usual—Kritten gestured with the head of the axe that it would be safe for the Overworlder to rise.

The Overworlder glanced longingly over Kritten's shoulder, and the advisor saw that the intruder had noticed that they'd intentionally put themself between the stranger and the obsidian portal. The piglin wasn't quite ready to let the intruder race off yet.

Kritten pointed the axe at the Overworlder with purpose and hoped that they would figure out what they wanted. "Give me what you've got!"

The intruder gave Kritten nothing more than a confused look and a helpless shrug. They didn't understand at all.

Instead they pointed at themself and said something. Kritten cocked their head to one side to listen to them carefully.

"Farnum," the Overworlder said. "Farnum."

Farnum. Kritten realized that must be the Overworlder's name. They pointed to their own chest with their free hand, never letting their axe lower for even a moment. "Kritten! Kritten!"

The Overworlder mimicked the name, mangling it only slightly in the attempt. "Krit-En."

"Close enough!" Kritten said. "Now: Give me everything you've got!"

The Overworlder—Farnum, Kritten corrected—shook their head, still unable to understand anything else the advisor said. Kritten sighed in exasperation. They didn't have the patience to teach this fool how to speak properly.

They considered taking them down then and there, if only to keep things simple. But Kritten was tired and aching and didn't know exactly where they were, how they would manage to get out of there, and how to find someplace safe to go if they actually pulled that off.

Killing Farnum seemed like a waste at the very least, and Kritten had so little left to them that they didn't feel like they should let anything go to waste. Frustrated, they sat down in front of the obsidian portal and glared at Farnum as if daring the Overworlder to try to escape.

It was around then that the strider came limping around the bend.

Kritten saw it before Farnum did, and they instantly wondered what the Overworlder would think of it. They hoped that Farnum wouldn't try to attack such a harmless beast, but if that happened, Kritten wasn't going to stop it. Let the Overworlder exhaust their strength on useless things.

Kritten reached out with their axe and pointed it at the incoming strider. It took Farnum a moment to figure out what the gesture meant, but eventually they followed the line of sight the weapon's handle indicated and spotted the strider coming right for them.

To Kritten's surprise, Farnum didn't scream or bolt in terror. Instead, they leaped up and down and clapped their hands in delight.

Kritten didn't understand this reaction at all. They just gaped at the Overworlder as they walked over to the strider and attempted to introduce themself to it.

Oddly, the strider seemed to respond in kind, just as curious about the stranger as it was about them. The two of them circled each other for a bit and grew closer with every rotation. Soon enough, the Overworlder realized that the strider was pale and shivering and let loose a wild exclamation of sympathy—something that was in short supply in piglin society.

Farnum came over to Kritten, their eyes wide and pleading. Despite the language difference, it was hard to misinterpret what the Overworlder wanted. Kritten gestured at the strider with their axe and then to Farnum, indicating that the Overworlder could take possession of the strider if they liked—even though the creature wasn't really Kritten's to give away.

Farnum practically squealed with glee. They were so excited that Kritten worried that they might burst. They spun about again and again until they were dizzy with delight.

When they were done, they fell over and collapsed on the ground and laughed themself silly. The strider approached to lean over the Overworlder and see if they were dead, which set Farnum off laughing again.

Once Farnum managed to recover from their joyousness, they began rummaging through their pack. That got Kritten's attention, and the advisor stood back up and brandished their axe at the Overworlder, warning them not to try anything stupid.

Farnum just put up their empty hands and smiled at Kritten until the axe was lowered. Then they went right back to picking through their pack, although much more gingerly this time. A moment later, they produced something surprising and reached out to Kritten with it.

The advisor looked at it suspiciously. It was a glass flask filled with a violet fluid and stoppered with a cork. They glared at it and shook their head.

The Overworlder sensed Kritten's misgivings. To allay any fears the advisor might have, Farnum uncorked the flask and took a little sip of the fluid themself. After a quick swallow, they opened their mouth and let loose a dramatic "Ah!" of refreshment. Then they offered the flask to Kritten again.

Still suspicious, but feeling a bit less cautious than normal, Kritten accepted the flask from Farnum. They put it to their lips, watching the Overworlder's reaction the entire time. Farnum didn't seem like someone excited about tricking a foe into drinking a bottle of poison. Instead they seemed entirely delighted.

Kritten took a sip of the viscous fluid. It went down slowly, but it tasted delicious. It filled them with a wonderful sense of warmth that seemed to permeate them all the way to their fingertips and the ends of their toes.

A moment later, Kritten had gulped down the whole thing without even meaning to. It was so good, and it made them feel incredible.

Farnum gestured toward the bruises they'd had on their arm, and they glanced down at them to see that they had disappeared. They were so surprised that they put down their axe so they could roll up a sleeve and get a better look at their arm. There was no longer any sign of an injury on it at all!

Kritten gaped at the Overworlder. They had heard about Potions of Healing like this, but the ingredients were hard to come by in the Nether. Apparently that wasn't the case wherever Farnum was from.

The advisor gazed up at the smiling Overworlder and realized that they hadn't even flinched toward attacking them, even though they were completely vulnerable. Kritten found that hard to believe, but in a gesture of goodwill on their own part they lowered their axe and bowed their head to Farnum to say thanks.

The Overworlder sighed in relief, and their smile grew even wider.

Meanwhile, the strider had become fascinated with the obsidian portal and walked within a couple feet of it, staring at it the entire time. Farnum moved to intercept the creature, unsure that it should be allowed to depart, but Kritten gestured toward the swirling portal as if asking them both to leave.

Perhaps that was foolish on the advisor's part, but they didn't see anything good coming from Farnum getting mixed up in their troubles here in the Nether. Kritten couldn't defend them from the other piglins and had nothing to trade with them now either. Better to send the Overworlder back home where they would be safe from the predations of the place's hostile mobs—and maybe they could return with more potions or other incredible things!

In an effort to encourage that, Kritten reached into their pack and produced a bit of warped fungus, something the advisor knew that striders were fond of. They handed it over with a grunt, and the Overworlder accepted it graciously.

Farnum followed the strider over to the portal cautiously, clearly not wanting to give Kritten the impression that they were trying to flee. The Overworlder even gestured for the advisor to join them on the other side of the portal.

For a moment, Kritten considered going with the Overworlder, but from what they had been told it was impossible for piglins to survive in the Overworld. If that wasn't true, Kritten felt sure the piglins would have invaded the place and conquered it long ago. Many piglin myths spoke about such great battles, but they all somehow skipped over both how the piglins had gotten into such places and what might have driven them back.

Instead, Kritten simply waved goodbye to Farnum and wished them well. The advisor was determined to figure a way out of the pit, but they didn't think Farnum would be much help to them in that regard. They would have to manage it on their own.

Farnum gave Kritten a *well, I tried* shrug and led the strider through the obsidian portal. With a spin of the purple energies swirling within, they were gone.

CELEBRATION

As Farnum emerged back in the Underworld with the strider by his side, he was awed by what had been far and away the most amazing thing that had ever happened to him. He never in his entire life thought that he would somehow wind up in the Nether. From everything he'd heard about it, it was the last place he'd ever want to be.

When he'd walked through the obsidian portal, he'd been desperate, despairing that he would ever find his way back to the Overworld. Now, after braving the Nether and coming back with a creature even more amazing than an axolotl, a sense of determination washed over him. If he could survive that—and apparently even make a new friend while doing it—then he could certainly figure a way out of here.

As he gazed around the place, though, he realized he had no idea how. For a moment, despair threatened to overwhelm him again. Then the strider nuzzled up next to him, knocking him out of his darkest thoughts. Even here, outside of the Nether, it seemed pale and shivering, but he didn't know what he could do to help with that. Instead, he gave the creature a friendly scratch along its top and took a moment to enjoy its company.

How wild to find such a creature. It would be the hit of the zoo!

If he could get both it and himself back there . . .

Farnum sat down and decided to go through his pack and see what kind of resources he had with him. Grinchard had insisted on putting the pack together for him, and Farnum had been all too happy to trust in his well-traveled pal's judgment. He'd tossed some of his favorite food and some other odds and ends in it before they'd started out, but otherwise he wasn't entirely sure what might be in it.

He took everything out of it a piece at a time and laid it out in front of himself in the glow of the obsidian portal. He found:

A torch (always handy, especially in the dark).

A set of flint and steel (which he'd already made good use of).

A bundle of food (still pretty full).

A bottle of water (which he topped off in the river).

A couple more Potions of Healing (just in case).

A couple more buckets (for capturing axolotls or other water-loving creatures).

A bed (which he hadn't even bothered to use during his nap the previous afternoon).

An iron sword (which he didn't really know how to use that well, but Grinchard had given it to him long ago).

A crafting table (because, hey, you never know what you might have to make for yourself on a long trip).

A wooden pickaxe.

Farnum stared at the last item in shock. He knew for sure he hadn't put that in there. Mycra must have slipped it into his pack at some point without telling him, maybe weeks ago. Otherwise, he would have objected for sure. After all, the thing he was most afraid of was having to tunnel through the Underworld.

Mycra wouldn't have seen it that way, though. As an experienced miner, she wouldn't understand how Farnum could possibly go off wandering in the wilderness without at least a cheap pickaxe in his pack. For her, that would have been like going for a hike without boots. You could do it, sure, but why?

Even touching the thing made Farnum shudder.

But he didn't see another way out of here. Not unless he could turn into a fish.

Still, he was determined to exhaust every other possibility first.

He reassembled his pack, leaving out the torch and the pickaxe. He gave the strider a bit of food, hoping to keep it too busy to wander off, and he lit the torch.

Then he walked around the entire edge of the cavern, just to make sure he actually was trapped there. Nothing would have pleased him more than finding another way out—at least one that was safe and dry.

He did figure out where the river left the cavern, but it did so by flowing out under the surface of the water. After having nearly drowned going over one Underworld waterfall, he didn't feel like tempting that particular fate again.

Especially not with the strider in tow.

Now that Farnum got a better look at the strider by torchlight, he realized the creature had been hurt. He supposed he should have noticed it limping before, but he'd been so astonished by everything in the Nether—including Kritten, who had seemed like they were going to kill him on the spot—that it had slipped by him.

He wasn't sure how well a Potion of Healing might work on the strider. After all, it was from the Nether, and things seemed to work very differently there. Of course, a potion had worked on Kritten, so maybe it would help after all.

He decided to risk it. He gave the strider a sip of one of his remaining Potions of Healing, and it seemed to perk the creature up. Throwing caution to the wind, Farnum fed the strider the rest of the bottle, and it chugged the entire thing down.

Only a moment after the potion was gone, the strider was galloping around the island in the cavern as if it had never been hurt at all. The sight made Farnum laugh with joy. He hated to see animals suffer, and he always tried to help them if he could.

Once the thrill of being healed so well wore off, though, the strider came back over to Farnum and nuzzled up against him again. For a moment, Farnum felt flattered, but then he realized the creature was shivering. It must have been trying to get close to him to get warm!

It was chilly in the cavern—much colder than it had been in the Nether. Farnum realized that if he didn't get the strider up to the surface and warmed up soon, he would have to send it back to the Nether for its own good.

There was only one way he could make that happen.

He hefted the pickaxe in his hand. It was a pretty shoddy one, just for use in emergencies, he supposed—and this looked exactly like an emergency to him. If it broke, he'd be stuck down here, maybe for good.

But if he didn't even try, the same thing would be true.

No matter how much it scared him, he had to give it a shot.

He walked over to the closest edge of the cavern, right next to the island, and he started digging upward as fast as he could.

THROUGH THE PORTAL

Kritten sat and stared at the obsidian portal for a long time. They knew that they should just leave it alone and go find a way out of the pit. The fact that there had been a strider down here—which now seemed like it had been uninjured until the advisor had landed on it—implied that there might be some sort of escape.

Besides the one that they'd spent so long staring at, of course.

Curiosity had always driven Kritten throughout their life. Other piglins liked to call Kritten smart, but the truth was that the advisor was insatiably curious. They wanted to know everything about everything.

To Kritten, knowledge was power.

To most piglins, *muscle* was power, but Kritten had been short-changed in that category. Knowledge was the only way they knew to get ahead, and the best part was that they could always find more of it. Eventually you couldn't get any stronger, but nothing could stop Kritten from learning more.

The obsidian portal represented the most incredible source of knowledge that Kritten had ever encountered. It also seemed like the most dangerous.

The Overworld was reputed to be toxic to piglins. As far as Kritten knew, they might die the moment they stepped through that swirling purple field.

But really, there was only one way to find out.

Eventually Kritten got tired of trying to talk themself out of doing it and just gave in. They stood up, squared off against the portal, and willed themself to walk through it.

The fact their feet refused to move toward it surprised them.

Kritten hadn't realized they were so attached to living. They'd taken a lot of risks earlier in life when they'd helped Bungus rise through the piglin ranks. Apparently they'd gotten too comfortable living in the bastion.

That was going to have to change.

Kritten forced their feet to move forward one grudging step at a time until their nose was just inches away from the obsidian portal. The swirling purple filled the whole of their vision so that it seemed like there was nothing else in the entire world.

As much as their body rebelled against moving forward, Kritten forced it to lean forward inch by inch until the tip of their nose finally brushed up against the spinning field.

And then they were somewhere else.

Kritten stumbled and nearly fell as they appeared on the other side of the obsidian portal, but they managed to catch themself before they tumbled into the river beyond. The very sight of that much liquid made Kritten gasp, though, and they fell to their knees to gawk at it.

In the Nether, liquid like this simply didn't exist. The potion that Farnum had fed the advisor had been more liquid than they had ever seen in one place in their life. The idea that there could be so much of it, enough to fill an entire cavern like this, staggered Kritten.

What an amazing world! To think that the piglins might be able to come here and conquer even this single cavern, what would that mean to them? To be able to have this much liquid whenever they wanted it?

The thought made Kritten dizzy and began to curdle their stomach. They tried to stand up, and they quickly concluded that it wasn't the wild possibilities of this world that was making them feel ill.

It was the world itself—or something lacking in it.

This was the problem that Kritten had read about. The Overworld was not meant for piglins like them. If they didn't return to the Nether soon, they would succumb to the illness and might even die.

As incredible as this place was, it wasn't worth Kritten's life. They turned around to head back through the obsidian portal before it was too late.

In the purple glow of the portal's field, though, Kritten saw something even more amazing than the water: ancient markings. Images left there that seemed to tell the story of a piglin invasion!

Someone, at some long-forgotten point in time, had come here from the Nether—probably through this very same obsidian portal—and scratched some diagrams on the cavern walls in a series of foot-high pictures. The images covered the wall for blocks in either direction, and Kritten couldn't take it all in at once.

From the bits that they could see from where they stood,

the images showed several similar figures—piglins perhaps—charging across a landscape and attacking a strange collection of foes. Kritten could pick out at least four different types of defenders, including some that looked like the skeletons that roamed the Nether. Above them all stood a lone hero—maybe an Overworlder like Farnum, only far stronger, of course—holding aloft some sort of weapon and leading the defense. A large block—the prize they were fighting over?—hung over the entire scene, radiating power.

Was this the story of a mighty piglin army that had once invaded the Overworld—just as had been spoken of in piglin legends? Kritten couldn't be sure.

Did it tell what had happened to those long-ago piglin warriors? Did it explain how they managed to invade the Overworld without the poisonous environment making them ill? The swirling questions made Kritten wonder how they might be able to put the answers to use.

They didn't know. They bent over and threw up instead. They had to get out of here as soon as possible or all the knowledge in this world or the Nether wouldn't be any good to them.

Kritten staggered toward the obsidian portal. This time they plunged through it without any hesitation whatsoever.

As Kritten emerged into the Nether, relief washed over every inch of them from head to toe. The feeling of impending doom vanished, although the queasiness in their stomach remained. Exhausted by the experience, they lowered themselves to the floor of the pit, sprawled out across it, and simply focused on breathing air meant for their lungs until the awfulness of the whole experience began to leave them.

The moment that Kritten felt better, they sat up and gave the obsidian portal a hard stare. The field inside of it didn't respond at all. It just kept on swirling like nothing had ever disturbed it.

While the portal might not have been changed by the experience, Kritten had. They didn't care how sick a trip through the portal made them. They were going to go back through and decipher the piglin message left on that wall no matter what.

As long as Kritten didn't stay on the other side for too long, it seemed like they could recover from such ventures. If they were careful about it, they could go back and forth between the two worlds as often as they liked, with little to worry about other than a temporarily tender belly. They vowed that they would continue to do this over and over again until they managed to crack open the mysteries that the ancient images held.

And then, armed with that incredible knowledge, they would figure out just what to do with it.

STRIDING HOME

Farnum wasn't quite sure how he made it to the surface. He was so terrified the entire time that he wasn't sure he wouldn't just stop breathing at some point. Instead, he just kept digging and climbing and digging and climbing until he felt the sun on his face once more.

The strider came along behind him every step of the way as if it had been his pet since birth. Farnum wasn't sure if it was because it had become so attached to him or because it didn't want to be trapped in the Underworld any more than he did, but he felt better having it along, despite how much the creature shivered.

He wondered if the strider would have been better off back in the Nether. It hadn't looked all that healthy there either, though. He supposed if it wanted to it could have turned back for the portal at any time, but it stuck with him instead. He felt incredibly grateful for that.

The worst part of Farnum being trapped in the Underworld

when he was young had been the awful solitude of it all. The feeling that he was trapped there all by himself and would die there all alone and that no one might even ever find him and he'd be entombed in solitude like that for all time.

Having the strider by his side helped push those resurgent fears away. In fact, they helped spur him on. He couldn't just stop and feel sorry for himself at any point in the process of excavating himself, as that would have meant watching the strider suffer there with him. And he just couldn't stomach that.

When Farnum made it to the surface, the first thing he did was bring the strider up after him and give it a big hug to celebrate their victory over all that rock and dirt that had stood between them and freedom. The creature wasn't able to hug him back, of course, but it nuzzled up next to him, still shivering.

"We need to get you to the zoo right away so I can figure out how to help you," Farnum said, and he set straight out to do that.

Fortunately, it seemed like he had come out of the Underworld on the same side of the mountains on which he and his friends had started, which meant all he had to do was figure out which direction town was from there. He set out directly away from the mountains, and as they receded behind him he began to recognize landmarks on their face that seemed familiar. He realized he was a bit farther south than he needed to be, so he corrected course.

When he came upon a set of minecart tracks that ran directly away from the mountains, he literally cheered out loud. This close to town, he knew they had to lead back there. All he had to do from this point was follow them.

He wondered what had happened to Mycra and Grinchard. Had they somehow become trapped in that cave too? Did they realize that he'd gotten swept away in the river or not? Were they still looking for him?

He didn't know about any of that, but he did know the strider was suffering. He needed to take care of it first, and then he could go looking for his friends. Maybe he could even rally a search party to help him find them before they got into as much trouble as he had. The idea of him saving someone else for once heartened him.

He told himself that he was probably worrying for nothing. The others were experienced travelers, and there was probably nothing out there that the two of them couldn't handle, with or without him. Farnum's big mistake had been getting separated from them in the first place. If they'd all stuck together instead of wandering off separately, he would have been fine. They all would have.

Night was falling as Farnum finally made it into town. As he approached, he saw some sort of gathering happening in the main square. He'd intended to head straight for the zoo to get the strider settled in and taken care of, but he was too curious about what could be happening in the square to just ignore it.

So many people were gathered in the square that Farnum couldn't see who was in the center of it all and what they were talking about. He stood on his tiptoes and craned his neck to try to figure it out, but too many others blocked his way.

As he stood there, though, the strider began letting out a low moan that the people nearest to Farnum could not ignore. They side-eyed the strange creature and Farnum and sidled away to give them ample space. Farnum took advantage of this by edging forward a bit more, and the process repeated itself with a fresh group of visitors.

Moments later, Farnum found himself standing at the front

edge of the crowd, with the strider right next to him. As he emerged from behind the last row of townsfolk blocking his view, he saw that the folks in the center of the square were none other than Mycra and Grinchard, and they were trying to convince the village's mayor to help them gather a search party.

"It's crucial that we find him before the sun sets again, or he may suffer or even die of thirst," Grinchard said.

"Let's just hold on for a moment." The mayor put up her hands, asking for calm. "It's not like people don't wander off into the wilderness to explore from time to time. There's no reason to panic."

Despite that, Mycra wasn't having any of the mayor's excuses. "Do you have any idea who you're talking about? He's been avoiding any chance of being trapped underground since we were kids. This is *Farnum* we're talking about!"

Grinchard gave Mycra a gentle elbow in the ribs. "Do you mean *that* Farnum?"

The explorer pointed right over at the zookeeper and the amazing animal he'd brought with him, and Farnum gave his goggle-eyed friends a half-embarrassed wave. Mycra gasped, and the entire crowd gasped with her.

The mayor clapped her hands together and dusted them off as if she'd just completed a long day's work. "See?" she said. "Nothing to worry about, and no reason to panic."

Most of the crowd dispersed at that point, heading back to their homes and shaking their heads at all the commotion over nothing at all. Others flashed understanding smiles at Farnum and his friends, relieved to see that Farnum was back safe and sound and looking little worse for wear. Mycra and Grinchard stormed over to Farnum and locked him up in a massive group hug.

Mycra grabbed him by the shoulders and inspected him for injuries. "You had us so worried!"

Grinchard chuckled with a rueful shake of their head. "We almost had the entire town ready to dig up half the mountain looking for you. We're just glad you're okay."

"What happened to you?" Mycra seemed satisfied that Farnum was physically okay at least, but she was still terribly concerned for him. "We heard you shouting and then nothing. We scoured that entire cavern looking for you."

Farnum braced himself to launch into the entire story, but the strider interrupted him with a deep shudder and a low moan. Farnum reached out to comfort the creature and told the others, "I'll tell you the whole thing while we get this guy to the zoo."

The others agreed with a round of nods, and they all hustled over to Farnum's place. As they strode along, Grinchard stared at Farnum's new friend. "Is that a strider? Where did you find one of them? I thought they were native to the Nether!"

Farnum liked the respect he saw in his friend's eyes. "It's a long story," he said with a nod.

Despite that, it didn't take him too long to tell it. By the time the three of them—plus the strider—reached the zoo's gates, Farnum had told his friends everything about his inadvertent adventure.

Grinchard blew out a long, relieved sigh. "You're one lucky zookeeper. You could have died at so many points today!"

Mycra kept shaking her head in disbelief. "Going over an underground waterfall! Activating an obsidian portal! Entering the Nether! Meeting a piglin who didn't try to kill you!"

"And bringing back a strider alive!" Grinchard clapped Farnum on the back. "Good on you!"

Farnum grinned as he escorted them all into the zoo. He wasn't used to getting such praise from his far braver and more accomplished friends, and he liked it. "Thank you," he said. "I'm sorry I put you all to such trouble, what with gathering a search party and all, but I really appreciate it. I knew you wouldn't abandon me."

"Never," Mycra said. Grinchard gave Farnum a firm nod of agreement.

"I'm just happy to be home." Farnum turned and regarded the strider. "But now we need to figure out what's wrong with my new pal here."

The strider shuddered again, this time for much longer.

"He seems cold," Mycra said. "Let's light him a fire."

Farnum escorted the strider to an empty pen, and Grinchard built a fire next to the creature. Soon it was roaring and kicking off a searing heat, and the strider edged closer to it until it was almost touching the flames. Instead of moaning like it had been, it grunted in improved comfort.

"That seems to help, but he still looks cold," Farnum said. "The fire might not be enough."

Grinchard stuck a finger into the air as an idea struck them. "The Nether is full of lava. Striders like this one here can actually walk across it without being hurt, much less getting incinerated. We could probably put him right on top of this fire!"

Farnum looked back at the strider and saw that the creature had already worked its way nearly on top of the fire. The trouble was that it was starting to smother it.

"He seems happy enough for now, but that's not going to last for long. We need a more permanent solution if he's going to stay here."

"Or what?" Mycra gazed wide-eyed at Farnum like he was babbling utter nonsense. "You're going to bring him back to the Nether to set him free?"

"I think I know what would work," Grinchard said. "Lava."

Farnum cocked his head in confusion. "So I *should* bring him back to the Nether?"

Grinchard laughed. "The Nether isn't the only place you can find lava, you know. There's plenty of it underground, if you know where to look."

"Ooh! And I do!" Mycra started for the exit. "I'll be right back!"

While Mycra was gone, Farnum tried to get the strider to eat something. It turned up its nose at most of the food he offered it, but it finally begrudgingly ate some mushrooms he found in the corner of the zoo's feed shed.

Watching the strider munch on the mushrooms reminded Farnum that he hadn't eaten for far too long himself. Grinchard followed him into his kitchen and insisted that he sit and rest while they cooked up a delightful dinner.

The two of them were just settling down to eat it when Mycra showed up, dusting off her hands. "And that's that," she said as she sat down at the dining table. "Dinner looks great!"

"How's the strider?" Farnum asked, concerned.

"Much better now." She grinned at her friends. "I built him a fireproof tub and hauled up enough lava to fill it to the brim. He's wallowing in it right now like a pig in mud."

"Thank you." Farnum raised his glass. "To friends who are always there for you. No matter what."

"To friends!" the others said as they all clinked their glasses together.

THE DISCOVERY

I t took Kritten more time than they cared to think about, but
eventually they figured out what the ancient piglins had
carved into the wall of that mysterious cavern, and it stunned
them to their core.

Deciphering images like these wasn't an exact science. The
drawings could mean different things when matched with other
things, and Kritten didn't understand much about the historical
context necessary to interpret that. As best they could tell, there had
been three factions of invaders, and it seemed like they'd been un-
stoppable. Together they had conquered everything in their path.

The only thing the advisor couldn't understand was—if they
had in fact been piglins—how they'd done it. For such a mighty
force of piglins to invade the Overworld, they must have first figured out a cure for the poisoning that affected them when they
left the Nether to plunder this ripe and wonderful place.

The drawings showed three different hordes of what Kritten
believed were piglins. The images of the first featured motion

lines that showed them moving around at top speed, able to race past the others and dash around even their foes.

The drawings of the second horde showed them clustered around half-finished structures that looked a lot like the piglin bastions crumbling back in the Nether. The way some of the invaders were hauling blocks up to the others, it seemed as though they were building these bastions, fresh and new. In Kritten's mind, this confirmed that the creatures were piglins, as no others built such places—at least that the advisor knew about.

Squiggly lines arose from the members of the last horde. The advisor couldn't be sure what these represented, but from the way the horde's foes—and even friends—fled from those squiggles, they had to stand for something powerful. Perhaps those piglins had been incredibly smelly, to the point where their stench drove their foes from their presence? Kritten wasn't quite sure they'd gotten that part right, but they couldn't come up with a better guess.

In one section of the mural, Kritten spied an image of what seemed like a massive piglin carrying an incredible weapon: a spiked block swinging about on the end of a chain. The drawing sat near the bottom of the mural, and someone had drawn an arrow from it that pointed straight down toward a lump in the ground. Curious, Kritten dug into the lump and uncovered a chain! They kept digging, following the chain, until they unearthed the entire thing: a vicious weapon that looked much like the one on the wall!

For Kritten, this discovery reinforced the story the drawings seemed to be trying to tell. This might not be just some fanciful tale but an actual legend!

They inspected the weapon and discovered that the block at the end of it was made of dark metal. It was just the kind of weapon that any piglin would covet. The advisor tested it out, swinging it around. After nearly hitting themself in the head, they decided that such an unwieldy weapon might not be for them. At least not yet.

For Kritten, the mural combined with the weapon seemed to confirm several such legends that they'd heard before, but they also brought up more questions than they answered. If the piglins had once conquered the Overworld, how had they fallen so low? What had kicked them out of the Overworld and back into the Nether? Had they been driven out by some powerful force, or had they somehow turned on one another instead?

Had the cure for Overworld poisoning failed them, or had something else been at work? Something that had driven the piglins permanently from that land?

Those last questions plagued Kritten's every thought. Had something gone wrong with the ancient piglins' solution for that awful poisoning?

Or could Kritten replicate their solution?

Or maybe find another way to avoid it?

There was only one way to figure all this out, as distasteful as it seemed. They didn't have the resources they needed here in the pit to survive for long much less for doing deep research. Because of that, they had no other choice. They were going to have to sneak back into Bungus's bastion.

Getting out of the pit didn't turn out to be nearly as difficult as Kritten had feared. It turned out that the strider had simply walked down into the place from a passageway hidden behind the obsidian portal.

To Kritten's embarrassment, it had taken them a while to figure this out. The active portal had blocked the sight of it, and for the longest time the advisor had not thought to look behind it. Instead, they'd set out to follow the wall of the cavern, just like they had before, and they'd gotten all the way around the entire place before they saw what they'd been missing.

Perhaps the ancient piglins had used the passageway as a means to get from Bungus's bastion to the obsidian gate and from there to the other world. It seemed lucky that the strider hadn't accidentally wandered through the portal itself.

Maybe the portal hadn't been activated when the strider entered the cavern? Or maybe the silly animal had wandered into the portal and back out again? Unless it returned to the Nether and suddenly developed the ability to talk, Kritten would likely never know.

Putting that question aside, the advisor followed the passageway behind the obsidian portal up and around and through many blocks of rock until it eventually came out not into the open Nether but into an underground room that Kritten didn't recognize at first. After a bit of exploration, though, the advisor confirmed their suspicions that it was in fact a chamber in the basement of the Great Bungus's bastion.

Of all the places for Uggub to hurl Kritten into, it turned out that it featured a secret passage back to the bastion!

The ancient piglins had been much smarter than Kritten could have imagined, with much greater foresight. When Kritten thought about how piglins like the Great Bungus and Uggub were now in charge of their people, it almost broke their heart to think of how the piglins had fallen so far.

That made them even more determined to do something about that injustice.

If Kritten didn't know about this secret basement room,

chances were good that few of the bastion's current residents did either. With a bit of luck and cunning, the advisor might be able to sneak around the place without anyone being the wiser. After all, Bungus's soldiers were looking for Kritten outside of the bastion, not *inside* it.

Kritten drew their axe and went looking for what they needed. They found their way into the vast storehouse under the bastion in which the piglins kept their food. There they filled their pack, this time with the best food they could find, and they stuffed their pack with plenty of other supplies.

As they were doing this, Kritten heard the one thing they'd really been hoping for: snoring.

Kritten knew that some of the lowliest and laziest piglins in the bastion liked to shirk work by hiding down in the storerooms. Bungus often railed against such slackers and ordered Uggub to root them out and exile them into the Nether—just as they'd done to Kritten. They were generally too clever for Uggub to find them though.

But not too clever for Kritten.

They moved aside a loose chest in a stack of them and slipped past it to a makeshift hideout on the other side. There Kritten found a pair of greasy young piglins who had likely never done an honest day's work in their lives. The shocking part was that Uggub hadn't been able to find them by their stench alone, surrounded as they were by rotting scraps of food and filthy clothing and bedding.

The two piglins appeared to have passed out after overindulging in stolen food. Kritten nudged one of them with a boot and got nothing from them but a more irritated—and irritating—snore.

Kritten fished a length of rope out of their pack and put the edge of their axe against the neck of one of the piglins. Then they jabbed the sleeping piglin in the throat with it until they woke up with a squeal.

Kritten handed the wide-eyed and trembling piglin a length of rope. "Tie your friend up with this. If you wake them up while you do it, that will be the last mistake you ever make."

The terrified piglin nodded silently and tried to stifle their snuffling as they followed the advisor's orders. In mere moments, they had their companion's hands bound in front of them and their ankles hobbled together.

Kritten handed them another length of rope. "Now your ankles."

When they were done, Kritten inspected the work and made them do it over, properly this time. The advisor wasn't sure if the slacker was trying to prepare for an eventual escape or was just lousy at tying knots, but they supposed it didn't matter in the end.

After some potentially painful — well, not for the advisor — negotiations, Kritten managed to get the slacker's hands bound too and then inspected all the knots on both of the piglins. They would do for now.

Then they woke the sleeping slacker — who was shocked to discover their new situation — and led the pair of prisoners out of the storeroom and into the basement room with the secret door. Soon enough they made it back to the bottom of the pit, where the obsidian portal still swirled at them, beckoning them to enter.

The prisoners had been trembling in fear the entire march down there, but now their legs gave out underneath them. This suited Kritten just fine. They took one of the piglins and bound them to an outcropping of rock next to the obsidian portal. Then they took the other one, hauled them to their feet, and gave them one end of a good length of rope.

Kritten jabbed the hapless prisoner with the end of their axe. "Now go through that portal and stay there on the other side! If you come back through there before I tell you to, I'll chop you in half on the spot!"

"No!" the piglin bound to the rock said. "Don't do it!"

Kritten kept their axe and eyes on the piglin in front of them but spoke to the other one. "If they refuse, I'll get rid of them and then send you in there instead!"

The other piglin gasped in horror and then spoke to their friend, their voice cracking with every word. "Well then, what do you have to lose?"

The piglin with the axe at their chest scowled at their faithless friend and then nodded at Kritten. "Fine! I'll do it!"

With that, the piglin turned to face the obsidian portal and — without any ceremony or further hesitation—walked right through the purple field, trailing the length of rope behind them.

Kritten grabbed the loose end of the rope and held it up off the ground. To their amazement, the other end of it remained hanging in the middle of the portal's purple field, even though the rest of it was now in another world.

Kritten waited for a good long time to see what would happen next. They figured that the piglin in the cavern would eventually get scared by the poisoning and come back through the portal, at which point the advisor would have to stab them to prove to the other piglin that they meant what they said.

To Kritten's amazement, the rope remained hovering in the portal—right up until it abruptly sagged downward.

Frowning, Kritten put down their end of the rope and followed it through the portal, keeping their axe ready before them. On the other side, they found the piglin collapsed on the island. They were unconscious but still breathing.

Not wanting to spend any more time in the poisonous world than they had to, Kritten returned to the Nether and hauled on the rope until the unconscious piglin blipped over into the Nether as well.

"Oh, no!" The other piglin began to snuffle in horror at their friend's fate. "What are you doing?"

Kritten bound up the knocked-out piglin and then turned their full attention to the other. "Learning."

THE ZOO STAR

"**W**elcome, welcome, welcome!" Farnum said to the crowd that had gathered outside the zoo's gates. After all the preparations that he and his friends had made for the strider's habitat, it was finally the day to open that part of the zoo to the public and give people a chance to meet the strider for themselves.

Even with his friends' help, it had taken Farnum more than a week to get everything in order, and he'd had to shut down the zoo for that entire time. Meanwhile, in their off hours, he'd gone around to every public place in the entire town and told people about the wonderful things they'd been doing and how amazing the strider would be to see. He hoped he'd been able to drum up some interest by talking it all up, but until he came out that morning to open the gates, he hadn't realized how successful he'd been.

There had never been so many people who wanted to enter the zoo at once. For the first time ever, Farnum had to say the words, "Would you please make a line."

Normally he just let people in as they wished, but so many of them wouldn't fit in the place at once—not without potentially scaring all the animals. He didn't want to risk that, especially not when it was the strider's first day being introduced to the public.

"Come on in, one at a time, please. Stay to the left and follow the wall around to the right. You'll be able to see all of the animals and spend plenty of time with them."

He shaded his eyes and looked out at the people who had politely lined up at his request. They maybe didn't speak the same language, but they seemed to have understood him all the same. There were a few of them he didn't recognize at all, and he wondered if they'd actually come here from outside town just to see his zoo! Had the zoo become a tourist attraction?

"This is amazing," Farnum said to Mycra as she approached him and patted him on the shoulder. "Look at all these people!"

"Congratulations!" She favored him with a proud smile. "You worked hard at this."

"We all did! Thank you—and Grinchard too. I couldn't have done any of this without you."

"Maybe you should thank us *after* you go check out the strider's pen," Mycra said with a small wince.

She didn't need to say another word. She just shooed him away and took over watching the door for him. He trotted over to the new attraction's pen.

He and his friends had done an amazing job with it, he had to admit. Not only had they reinforced the pen both to keep the strider from wandering off and to protect it from outside mobs, they'd built a pool of lava for the strider to enjoy at all times.

That had taken lots of work. Grinchard had helped find a source of lava, and the three of them had then brought it to the zoo, bucket by bucket.

Farnum had worried that bringing lava into the zoo might be

dangerous—and he still wasn't convinced that it was actually safe—but it had made the strider so happy. The creature had been so excited that Grinchard had volunteered to help train it so that it could work off some of its excess energy and become happy in its new home.

Farnum hadn't been able to argue against logic like that—or against the results. He had never seen the strider in such a good mood, and it seemed healthy as could be. Thriving, even.

And then he walked into the strider part of the zoo and found Grinchard riding the creature.

The adventurer had somehow come up with a saddle and strapped it atop the strider like it was a mount, and now they were riding it across the surface of the pen's lava pool. Despite the saddle, Grinchard didn't seem to have any control over which way the creature trotted, but it wasn't like there was a massive amount of room in the pen anyhow. The explorer just grinned as they rode the strider all around the pen at random.

The zoo's visitors had all stopped to gape at the sight, which helped explain why traffic had backed up at this part of the zoo.

Farnum opened his mouth to yell at Grinchard and order them to get off the strider and back on this side of the fence's pen where they belonged. And then something shut him up.

He couldn't say exactly what stopped him. Maybe it was the way the visitors goggled at the sight, something he'd rarely seen happen in the zoo till that day. Maybe it was how content the strider seemed to be with a rider on its back, encouraging it to traipse back and forth across the lava in whatever direction pleased it.

Or maybe it was the goofy smile on his friend's face.

"They're having a ball out there."

Farnum turned to find Mycra at his shoulder, watching the

wild show in the pen and laughing along with the crowd. She nodded toward Grinchard. "Don't you think?"

"I wasn't sure if you meant the strider or the person riding it."

"Fair." Mycra chuckled. "You know, if Grinchard had a fishing rod with a warped fungus dangling from the end of it, I bet they could get that strider to go where they wanted it to, rather than just having it wander around at random."

"I actually have some of that! The piglin I met in the Nether gave it to me, maybe for that exact purpose! I'll have to mention that to Grinchard when they're done," Farnum said, laughing. "Just not quite yet."

"Maybe we should set the two of them up to do this sort of thing on a regular schedule. Give the visitors something to look forward to—and maybe spread out the crowd a little bit too."

"That's not a bad idea at all." Farnum scratched his chin. "And it might keep Grinchard around for a bit longer too before they get bored and wander off again."

Mycra put a hand on his shoulder. "They always come back. We both do. Do you know why that is?"

Farnum shrugged, not quite getting where this was leading. "To resupply, I always figured."

"Sure, that's part of it. You want food and drink and fresh clothes and equipment and all the other things you need to survive out there in the wild world. But after many days and nights alone, that's not what draws you back. Not really."

Farnum narrowed his eyes at Mycra, who never let her gaze wander from Grinchard having so much fun atop that strider. Not for an instant.

"It's the need to know you're not alone. Even when you're out there for days or weeks or months at a time. Not really."

Farnum finally got it. "You're always welcome back here. I'll keep the home fires burning for you both."

Mycra laughed gently at that. "It'll be a lot easier to manage that now that you've got all that lava right here."

"That it will."

DISCOVERED

Kritten's experiments had borne fruit. After sending the two captured piglins through the portal time and again, the advisor had determined the rough amount of time a piglin could survive in that poisonous world before succumbing entirely.

It wasn't long.

Fortunately, neither of the piglins had perished, and both of them had recovered quickly once returned to the Nether. Kritten wasn't sure if that was because the Nether had some sort of healing property for piglins or the other world lacked something the piglins sorely needed, but they supposed that was just a matter of definitions.

The next step was figuring out if there was some way to protect the piglins from the effects of visiting that other world.

Kritten had a scant few leads to go on. The ancient legends scrawled on the wall in that cave on the other side of the portal seemed to indicate that Nether wart played an important role in the solution, but it didn't seem like those drawings ever showed exactly how that worked.

Neither of the piglins who had been forced to walk through the obsidian portal had lasted there nearly as long as Kritten had during their research visits. While Kritten had a decent enough ego about their intelligence, they didn't think there was anything special about them physically. The other piglins should have been able to withstand the sickness over there much better than the advisor had.

So what was the difference?

Kritten suspected it was a lingering effect of the Potion of Healing that Farnum had given to them. Perhaps the potion had imbued them with some sort of protection that kept the illness away.

Reluctant to endure such experiments on their own person while they already had other perfectly decent subjects at hand, Kritten nevertheless returned through the portal to see how long they lasted now. It had been days since they'd been back there, and any residual effects of the potion should have long ago faded away.

Despite that, when Kritten walked into the cave, they didn't get sick. Not right away. Not like the other piglins, at least.

But faster than before.

Had the Potion of Healing only partly worn off? That seemed unlikely after so much time.

Maybe there was something else at work. Something that Kritten hadn't been paying attention to.

The advisor took off their pack and emptied their pockets, laying everything out on the ground before them. Nothing there looked like it would be particularly effective as proof against what the Overworld did to piglins, but Kritten knew that they had to put aside their assumptions and give it a shot anyway.

They took a deep breath and walked into the Overworld again.

It turned out that their theory was correct. They became sick almost instantly and were forced to return to the Nether in record time.

While that had felt horrible, this was good news. It meant two things.

First, if a Potion of Healing could offer a residual bit of protection from the illness for a short while, then perhaps something else—one concocted specifically to counteract the poisonous effects of the Overworld—might offer longer-term protection.

Perhaps even permanent.

That seemed unlikely, though. If piglins could be made to tolerate the Overworld permanently, why would the ancients who scrawled those pictograms on that cave wall ever have left that softer, easier world behind?

Second, whatever it was that was protection against the Overworld's effects, it seemed that Kritten had been carrying at least a little bit of it with them when they had gone into the Overworld the first time that day.

Inspired, they separated out everything they had put down before and began to pick up the things one at a time and carry them into the Overworld to see what would happen. At one point, they went into the Overworld and felt fine for a good few moments, much longer than normal.

It didn't last.

When Kritten returned to the Nether, they looked down at what they were holding in their hand: a chunk of Nether wart that they'd stolen from the bastion's basement.

Somehow this strange fungus—which grew all over the

bastion—had offered Kritten some protection. Maybe it had been an ingredient in the potion that Farnum had fed them.

The only trouble was that Kritten couldn't make a potion in the Nether. Liquids never lasted long in the Nether. If brought there from the Overworld and left unbottled, they evaporated almost immediately. The advisor would never be able to fashion such a thing here.

But they might be able to manage it in the Overworld.

Of course, to do that, they'd have to stay in the Overworld long enough to brew the potion, and they weren't quite sure how they'd manage that.

Still, Kritten now had some new information and something new to strive for—and two subjects to experiment on until they found the answers they sought.

Or the need for new subjects arose.

Kritten snuck back into the bastion and made off with a crafting table, several empty vessels, and as much Nether wart as they could carry. Then they set to work.

Nether wart was clearly the key. Fortunately, the Great Bungus's bastion had a plentiful supply of that.

What they didn't have a lot of were bottles. There wasn't a whole lot of demand for such things in the Nether, after all, where you couldn't find any liquid to put into them. Despite that, Kritten managed to find a few hidden away in a chest in the basement, things that may have once held potions long ago.

Had they been used by those ancient piglins in the drawings? The ones who maybe had built the bastion too? Or had someone bartered with Overworlders for them long ago and then thrown them down here once whatever had been inside them had been drunk?

Kritten was sure they would never know, but they were happy

to have found them either way. They also discovered a bucket stored with the bottles, and they swiped that too.

To start their experiments Kritten made a frame of Nether wart and hung it around their neck. To their delight, it gave them a good deal of time in the Overworld before they began to feel ill, and then much slower than before. Using this, they were able to haul the crafting table into the Overworld and get to work.

The first thing they did there was use their stolen bucket to scoop up some water from the river. It was surprisingly heavy, but Kritten managed to get it back to the crafting table where they could work with it.

Then they did something that no other piglin had ever done, as far as Kritten knew. They began brewing potions.

First Kritten made a supply of basic potions using Nether wart. Then they began adding other elements to the potions one at a time. When they had a wide assortment of potions ready, they hauled them back into the Nether, lined the bottles up, sat down in front of their piglin prisoners, and made them a proposal.

"As you might have realized by now, I'm trying to figure out how piglins like us can stand to be on the other side of that portal!"

The two piglins stared at the advisor, scared and confused. "Why would you want to do that?" one of them asked.

"Because the creatures over there are weak! The only thing protecting them from us is the way we get sick over there! If I can figure out a cure for that, we can storm right in and conquer the place!"

"That's impossible!" the other one scoffed.

The first one wasn't so sure. "You really think you can do that?"

Kritten nodded. "And if I do, the piglins who help me figure it out, they're going to be heroes! Right?"

The first one nodded and began to smile. "Right!"

"So, will you help me? I'm not going to force you to drink this stuff, but it would help if you'd try it!"

The second one squinted at the potion bottles. "Are they poison?"

The first one sneered at their friend. "Those are there to cure the poison, stupid!"

"I'm not stupid!"

"You are if you think those are poison!"

"Then I'll drink them!"

"No, I'll drink them!"

They both turned toward Kritten. "Me first!"

"No, me!"

Kritten smiled at them. "You'll both have a turn!"

The advisor loosed the bonds on both of the subjects and handed them each a potion to test. Once they drank it, Kritten prodded them through the obsidian portal.

The first few trials didn't produce much success at all. The subjects managed to tolerate their time in the Overworld for longer, but not for any real length of time. Still, this gave Kritten hope that they were on the right path, and they kept experimenting, despite the subjects' complaints of sour bellies and general exhaustion.

Eventually, after countless tries, Kritten came upon a formula for this vital potion that they believed was, well, if not correct, at least the best they could do at the time with the material at hand. But the subjects had become progressively sicker throughout the week, and they now weren't nearly as happy about all this as they had been when Kritten had launched this project with them.

The smart thing to do might have been to head back into the

bastion and procure a new subject or two, but Kritten worried that they might have already pushed their luck too far with their previous visits. As many things as they'd taken—not to mention the two current subjects themselves—someone was bound to notice. The advisor didn't want to increase the likelihood of that happening.

Instead, Kritten decided that the time to test the potion personally had finally come. They were healthier at the moment than either of the subjects, and—more to the point—Kritten needed to confirm the effects of the potion more than simple timing data would permit.

"Stay here," Kritten told the subjects while making final preparations for the experiment. "I shouldn't be gone too long."

Hoping to make that statement a lie, Kritten drank down the entire potion they had pinned all their hopes on, steeled themself for a moment as they felt it rush through them, and then stepped through the obsidian portal's swirling purple field.

The cavern looked exactly how they had left it. The river ran through it from the waterfall on one end to the point where it disappeared into the rocks again on the other. The pictograms on the wall loomed overhead, promising knowledge to those who could unlock their secrets. And the place felt far too cool for someone used to the Nether's relentless heat.

But it didn't make them feel ill!

Kritten sat down on the island and waited, monitoring their own body for any sign of sickness. The only thing that they felt was a rumbling deep in their stomach that reminded them that they had forgotten to eat for far too long.

That happened when they were engrossed in something like this. The needs of the body sometimes came after the needs of the mind. Kritten wondered idly if that was perhaps part of the reason the subjects had deteriorated so much. They were used to stealing as much food as they wanted whenever any appetite struck them, and the advisor only bothered to feed them when the need became too much for them to ignore.

But that was a problem that Kritten could address once they returned to the Nether. That was no reason to cut short this particular experiment. Not when it was going so well.

As they sat there, they noticed some movement in the river, and they froze. Could some kind of predator be swimming under the water? If so, how could it not drown?

There was a lot about this world that Kritten didn't understand—yet—and they didn't intend to let it be the end of them. They tensed their muscles, getting ready to flee.

Then the creature emerged from the water, and it was maybe the least threatening thing Kritten had ever seen. Its skin was pale, almost translucent, and it wasn't even half as long as the advisor's axe. It crawled about on spindly legs that seemed far better suited for the water, and it looked like even a strider could have taken it out with a single stomp.

Kritten laughed at their fears. While there was certainly much to learn about this strange world, not all of it was likely to be lethal. Farnum, for instance, had actually shown the advisor some kindness.

Kritten lay back on the island and closed their eyes for just a moment. It had been a long week, and they were tired. They'd pushed themself hard to develop the potion that might be the answer to all their troubles, and that had taken its toll.

The advisor wanted nothing more than to be restored to their chambers in the bastion. To sleep in their own room. Maybe, if this potion worked as well as they hoped, they could find a place to live in the Overworld instead.

Maybe they'd even run into Farnum again someday.

They awoke with a start and without any idea how long they'd been asleep. They cursed their mistake as they realized how lucky they were that they hadn't succumbed to the poisonous effects of this world and slumbered through their own death.

They checked themself and realized that they actually were feeling the effects of being in this world now. It wasn't much, just the start of things, but that had probably been enough to awaken them.

They needed to get back to the Nether fast.

They stood up and took a last glance around to see if they had forgotten anything. They noticed that the pale creature that had come up to greet them from the water was gone, but that was probably for the best. Then they strode through the obsidian portal, reminding themself to feed the subjects—or shout at them if they had caused any trouble during the advisor's absence.

The first thing Kritten noticed as they emerged into the Nether was that the subjects were gone. The advisor had left them sitting in front of the portal together, and they were no longer there.

Kritten started to wonder if the two hapless piglins had finally managed to escape on their own or if someone had helped them, and what that might mean for Kritten.

That all got cut short before the advisor could ponder it much further when the second thing that Kritten noticed leaped out of the shadows, knocked their axe from their hand, and plucked them up by their throat.

"Well, well, well," Uggub said with an evil chortle. "You've been a busy little piglin, haven't you?"

THINKING

Business had never been better at the zoo. Visitors came to check out the strider from all over the area, and it seemed like everyone in town had been there at least once if not twice. Farnum's friends had been so helpful at every point and so proud of him and so happy for his success.

But if he was honest with himself, the zoo's new sparkle was already starting to fade. He recognized it in the faces of the visitors who had seen everything that Farnum had to offer there and yearned for something new—and in the sighs of his friends as they took a moment every now and then to gaze toward the horizon with wistful expressions, thinking of the adventures that still awaited them out there.

Farnum had lived with the zoo being a failure for a long time, and he wasn't eager to go back to those days. Nor did he want his friends to leave for greener pastures again. Not yet, at least. He had to do something about that, and he knew just what it must be.

He had to return to the Nether.

There he could find something new for the zoo. Maybe he could even find those axolotls he'd been chasing after on the way. It didn't really matter, as long as he could bring something different back to his place and refresh the novelty of the zoo once again.

He thought about just sneaking out on his own and not telling anyone he was leaving, but he couldn't bring himself to do it. First of all, he couldn't just abandon the zoo to his friends like that, not after everything they'd done for him to help make it into what it was today.

Second of all, the Underworld still scared him, and the Nether was actually worse.

If he was going to go back there, he'd need some help.

He waited until the zoo was closed that night and they had finished eating and were relaxing before he brought the subject up. "I've been thinking," he started.

"Oh!" Mycra covered a smile and laughed. "I know *that* look. Although I don't know if I've ever seen it before on *you.*"

"I knew you had it in you," Grinchard said with a crafty smile. "It was always just a matter of time."

Farnum furrowed his brow at his friends, confused. "What in the Overworld are you two talking about?"

Mycra pointed straight at him. "Ambition!"

The word shocked Farnum. "What?"

"She's not insulting you," Grinchard said earnestly. "She's just pointing it out."

"I have ambition." Farnum opened his arms to encompass the entire zoo. "I mean, I built all this, right?"

"You did!" Grinchard said. "I mean, we helped, but we all help each other in all sorts of ways. This is yours—all yours—but until you brought that strider back with you it always seemed kind of, um, humble?"

Farnum wanted to demand that the adventurer explain himself, but he knew exactly what Grinchard meant. He'd had the same thoughts himself. He'd let his fears of the world beyond the edge of town keep him there and keep him focused only on animals he could find in the area.

He had wanted to bring back and feature more exotic animals, but he hadn't wanted to go find them himself. Sometimes his friends had come back from their travels and reported seeing all sorts of amazing creatures to him, but all that had done was whet his appetite. He'd never gone looking for them or even asked his friends to try to bring anything back for him.

Now, though, having finally had a taste of such things, he wanted to go back out and try it again—even though the first time had nearly been a fatal disaster.

Maybe that's why he still didn't feel good about venturing forth on his own. He wanted his friends by his side.

He decided to start over.

"I've been thinking."

Grinchard opened his mouth to interrupt, but Mycra quieted him with a steely glare.

"That the strider only represents the beginning of what I'd like this zoo to be. I'd like to bring in all sorts of new creatures to share with our visitors. To that end, I'd like to return to the Underworld to see what kinds of creatures we can find.

"I'd love to explore that cavern we found before I got swept up into the waterfall—and even the Nether beyond that. If the only thing stopping us is me, then—well—there's nothing stopping us."

The smiles on the others' faces dimmed when Farnum mentioned returning to the Nether. "You're not thinking of going back over that waterfall, are you?" Grinchard asked. "Even for seasoned pros like us, that's wildly dangerous."

Farnum knew that the *us* in that case meant his well-traveled friends and did not include him. "As far as I know, that's the only way to get back to the Nether, right? So I think we'll have to get back there eventually. I did dig a passage all the way back from there to the surface. I would *hope* we could find the top end of it again."

"Did you mark it somehow?" Mycra had a hopeful but doubtful note in her voice.

Farnum blushed. "I didn't think of it. I was just so relieved to be back in the Overworld!"

Grinchard waggled their head from side to side. "That makes it a bit harder but not impossible. There's a much easier way though. To get to the Nether, I mean."

"How's that?" Farnum didn't know much about the Nether outside of what he'd read in his books and the odd story here and there.

Mycra goggled at the explorer. "Seriously? You have to be kidding!"

Grinchard laughed off her concerns. "Why would I kid about something like that? I mean, just think about it. Look around the zoo. It would be so easy."

Farnum still had no clue what they meant. "What would be easy?"

"Easy?" Mycra arched an eyebrow. "To set up? Sure. But once you got it going?" She grimaced. "I don't know."

Farnum slapped his hands on the table to get the others' attention. "What are we talking about?"

"Building our own obsidian gate." Grinchard said it the same way Farnum might have suggested putting up a new animal enclosure.

"You can do that?"

Grinchard gave him a firm nod. "Can do. We could even put it right here in the zoo."

Farnum realized why Mycra had been staring at the explorer in shock, and he felt himself doing the same thing. "Is that wise?"

Grinchard chuckled. "I don't know about *wise*. It's probably wiser than hauling yourself back through your so-called Underworld to find the gate you already know about, though."

"How?" Farnum realized he was getting too excited and took a moment to steady himself. "I mean, how do you build something like that?"

To Farnum the portal he'd passed through seemed like some kind of monumental magic that had to have been built in ancient times by a mysterious people who'd long since been lost to history. The idea that anyone could just build one wherever they wanted seemed ludicrous.

"It's right there in the name," Grinchard explained. "*Obsidian portal.* It's really just a doorway made out of obsidian. You set it up and ignite it with fire, and boom! A portal to the Nether!"

"But where are we going to get that much obsidian? I've never seen that much of it in one place before."

Mycra sighed. "That's because you've never gotten too far out of town before. If you'd spent as much time mining as I have, you'd know it's not all that rare. I come across it in my job all the time."

Farnum felt his hopes rising. "So we just need to go out and gather enough obsidian to build the portal's frame? We can do that, right?"

Grinchard gave him a noncommittal shrug. "Sure. You could do it that way."

"If?"

"If you want to do it the hard way."

"What's the easy way?"

Mycra laid it out for him. "You can make your own obsidian. Right here."

Farnum found that hard to swallow.

"Obsidian is a volcanic rock. It's formed when lava cools quickly. Like when it runs into water."

"And we have a steady supply of lava right here in the zoo. . . ."

"Right," said Grinchard. "So we just add water—and presto! Obsidian!"

Farnum sat back in his chair, stunned. "And that's it? Why doesn't everyone have an obsidian portal in their backyard then?"

Mycra squirmed in her seat. "Well, it's not as easy as Grinchard makes it seem. For one, you can't mine obsidian without a diamond pickaxe, and those can be hard to come by."

"But you have one."

Mycra's lips curled up at the ends. "Of course. I *am* a professional."

"So that's not stopping us. What else?"

"If you build a gateway to the Nether, you have to be careful with it. If you can go through it from this side, things can come over from there too. And you can imagine how badly that can go."

"But if we're careful with it? If we shut it down when we're not using it?"

Mycra shrugged. "It's *safer*. But *safe*? Nothing's safe when it comes to the Nether."

"But for what we want to do?"

"It's safe enough," Grinchard said. "We can build it right here in the zoo to make sure no one comes by and activates it by accident."

Farnum scratched his chin. It sure sounded a lot safer than trying to find that other obsidian portal. And a lot more convenient too.

"All right. Let's do it."

SALVATION

Uggub hurled Kritten to the floor in the Great Bungus's throne room, bruising the advisor's knees along with their pride. "I found this lava-chewer skulking around a pit at the end of a secret passage from our storeroom! They've been stealing from us since they fled from your righteous anger!"

Bungus didn't look nearly as mad as the last time Kritten had seen them. Having had time to cool off, the piglin leader seemed more curious than anything else. "You always were a cunning little piglin! What have you been doing out there in the Nether?"

Kritten took a moment to stand up and dust off their clothing. Uggub immediately lost patience with them and shoved them back to the floor.

"I found the little traitor coming back through an obsidian portal!"

That got Bungus's attention. The leader sat back on his chair and marveled at the advisor. "Even after all this time, you never fail to surprise me! What did you discover on the other side of that portal?"

Kritten considered keeping the results of their explorations and experiments private, but they knew what that would lead to. If Uggub had their way, they'd throw Kritten off the top of the bastion this time and watch to make sure the vicious mobs in the Nether made a meal out of the results.

"I got to continue my work on a project that I know will be most important to you! And I would have completed it too if this fool hadn't interrupted me at the worst possible moment!"

Enraged, Uggub smacked Kritten across the back of the head and was preparing to do much worse to them, but the Great Bungus held up a hand to order the brute to stop. "Let them keep talking!"

Kritten snorted at Uggub and got up to dust their clothes off again. "The obsidian portal leads into a long-forgotten cave in the other world! And the walls there are covered with images that record the story of the legendary piglins who invaded that world so long ago!"

Bungus cocked their head at the advisor, intrigued but still suspicious. "Which legends?"

"You know the ones! We heard them when we were little! About how the great piglin warriors invaded a strange, bright land filled with easy battles and endless gold!"

The leader grunted in approval. "I do remember! A whole new land that we were banished from! And you found a way to reach it?"

It was Kritten's turn to be suspicious now, but there was no way out for them but forward, they knew. "Yes!"

Bungus's eyes grew wide with excitement, and he began to drool over the possibilities this news brought him. "Yes! This is just what I've been looking for!"

That statement thew Kritten off just a little bit. When they'd said that this research was important to Bungus, they'd just been trying to buy a bit more time. But now it seemed like they might have been more right than they knew. Rather than revealing their ploy, they waited for the Great Bungus to continue.

"This could be just what we need! We already conquered every piglin clan we can find around here! Now we're just sitting here getting fat and lazy and waiting for someone to become strong enough to rise up against us, or for someone to betray me. We need new things to conquer! If we can't find them in the Nether, then we should just leave the Nether behind!"

Kritten had to admit that Bungus had a point. The advisor had been thinking that sort of thing too, but they hadn't expected the leader to be so quick on the uptake. This was even better, though, as Kritten wouldn't have to explain the lure of it to Bungus at all.

Uggub tried to cool off Bungus's excitement. "It's not that simple! The world beyond ours is poisonous to us!" The brute stabbed a finger at Kritten. "This one kidnapped two of our people and forced them to enter that world over and over and over until they nearly died!"

Kritten turned about and saw that the two piglins they'd drafted into their research program were standing behind Uggub, looking a lot less ill than they had before. Rather than recoil from the advisor in fear as they'd been doing all week, they sneered at them instead.

With a snort Kritten confirmed Uggub's accusation. "I couldn't run all those experiments on myself! I used those two as volunteers to test my theories and come up with ways for us to tolerate being in the Overworld! I suppose Uggub would have volunteered for such tests and died on their first try!"

That sort of image put a smile on Kritten's face and a scowl on the brute's.

"They lie!" Uggub said. "They do nothing but lie!"

The Great Bungus considered everything that they'd heard. As Kritten knew, the leader couldn't be relied on to trust them fully anymore, no matter how much history they had between them. But the notion that Kritten had figured out a way for the piglins to escape from the Nether into a whole new world ripe for the plunder was simply too tempting to just throw aside.

The Great Bungus stood up and glared down at Kritten. "Show me!"

Kritten privately sighed in relief. At the very least, this would buy them more time before Bungus decided to have them executed. Uggub wouldn't make a move against them without the leader's blessing—or so Kritten hoped.

With Bungus and Uggub in tow—and Uggub's axe pointed at the advisor's back—Kritten led the way down to the bastion's storeroom. From there, they showed the entrance to the secret passage to Bungus, who grunted approvingly. The three of them proceeded down the passage until they reached the pit where the obsidian portal stood.

As they entered the cavern, Kritten moved off to one side and allowed the Great Bungus to marvel at the purple field swirling inside the doorway of polished black stone. Uggub, who had already seen all of this, kept a close eye on the advisor instead, watching and waiting for them to try something funny.

For their part, Kritten moved carefully, not wanting to give Uggub an excuse to smack them around or even to put an early end to them. They glanced around and saw that the brute had left their remaining stack of potion bottles untouched.

That meant Kritten still had a chance.

"This is the portal that leads to the Overworld?" Bungus eyed it suspiciously.

"It does! It first brings you into a cave in the underground portion of that world, and from there you can reach the surface! You just have to dig your way out!"

"Show me!"

Kritten moved toward the portal, but Uggub cut them off. "They're not telling you the whole truth, Great Bungus! If you go into the other world, it makes you sick!"

"I already said that!" Kritten protested. "Were you not listening? Or are you just stupid?"

Bungus cut them off with a chop of his hand. "But you have been working on a cure for this sickness?"

Kritten nodded. "I finally cracked the secret! It works well!"

"Do not drink anything they give you! It will be poison!" said Uggub. "You cannot trust them!"

"You cannot trust *Uggub*!" Kritten said to Bungus. "They have been undermining me ever since we took over the bastion! They only want to get me out of the way so they have a clear shot at overthrowing you and taking your power!"

"Enough!" the Great Bungus roared. "Kritten: You will take this cure of yours and divide it in half! Then you will take your portion of it first! Uggub: You will shut up!"

Kritten frowned. "I cannot make the cure here! It requires water!"

"You lie!" Uggub said. "There is no water here!"

Kritten pointed at the portal. "But there is over there! More water than any of us have ever seen! And I can make all the cure we need with it!"

"You cannot trust them!" Uggub protested.

Bungus backhanded Uggub across the chops. "Shut! Up!" The brute clamped their mouth shut but let their fury at their humiliation shine through their eyes.

The leader glared at Kritten, suspicious. "You will do this here!"

"I cannot! The cure evaporates almost instantly in the Nether!"

"You have a bottle of it ready here?"

Kritten nodded and pointed at one of the bottles sitting in front of the portal. "Just this one! We could both drink from it!"

"It's a trick!" Uggub said, although the brute clearly could not figure out how. They were just absolutely sure that Kritten could not be trusted.

When it came to protecting Kritten's life, they had to admit that Uggub was right. If they could have figured out a way to poison Bungus while drinking from the same bottle as them, they would have done it for sure.

"You go first!" Bungus said to Kritten.

The advisor hefted the bottle in front of them and then offered it to Uggub. "Unless you'd prefer to try it?"

The brute growled at Kritten but said no more. They had annoyed the Great Bungus enough already that day and didn't need to press it further.

"Go ahead!" Bungus said to the advisor. "Drink!"

"I will! But it would be better for us to go through the portal first so that you can feel the sickness for yourself!"

"Why would I do that?"

"If we drink the potions before we go through the portal, you will not feel the sickness at all! You might think the potion is pointless!"

Bungus nodded, understanding. They squinted at the smaller piglin. "And you want to show me how much I need it! And—by extension—need you!"

Kritten smiled in agreement. While their long-standing alliance with each other had frayed, they still followed each other well.

"Should I go through first? Or would one of you prefer the honor?" Kritten knew that the job of leading the three of them through *should* go to the advisor, but they also knew that if they insisted on it the others would dig their heels in against it.

Bungus gestured toward the obsidian portal with the back of a hand. "You may lead the way!"

Without further comment, Kritten strode right through the portal. The others came fast behind the advisor. Bungus didn't want to be left behind with such an amazing world to explore, and Uggub didn't want to let Kritten out of their sight for any time at all.

Kritten had been in the cavern countless times by this point and knew what to expect. They stood back and watched the other two marvel at their new surroundings instead. Uggub glanced around everywhere in utter suspicion, just waiting for something to attack them out of nowhere. The greedy Bungus looked like they might fall over in sheer amazement at the possibilities this opportunity presented.

Kritten was relieved to discover that their crafting table was still there. It wasn't like they couldn't have found another, but they'd been working so hard at it that they'd worried that something might have happened to it.

"While we're waiting, let me show you how I make the cure!" Kritten suggested.

"No tricks!" Uggub snapped.

Bungus, who was too busy being astonished at everything, simply waved for Kritten to go ahead with it.

Under the watchful eyes of Uggub, Kritten set about making

another bottle of the cure as quickly as they could. When they were finished, they corked it up and presented it to the others.

"It's that simple?" Bungus said, trying to appear as if they understood everything Kritten had done.

"You just need to know how to prepare all the ingredients in the right proportions and the right order!"

Bungus gave them a nod of approval. Uggub just grunted, sure that Kritten was preparing some kind of trick. The three of them stood there and waited for a long moment in uncomfortable silence.

This lasted until the poisonous effects of the world took hold upon all three of them. Uggub glared at Kritten, wanting to accuse them of somehow causing this problem. Bungus winced at the illness and pointed at the bottle in Kritten's hand.

"That seems like enough! I believe you about how this place affects piglins! Even ones as mighty as me! So, shall we drink?"

Kritten allowed themself a savage grin, then put their potion bottle to their lips and drank the whole thing in one gulp. When they were done, they threw the bottle on the ground—smashing it to pieces—and smacked their lips. "Delicious!"

Uggub groaned out loud, wanting to smack Kritten again but too ill to make the effort. "It's a trick!"

Bungus scowled at the advisor in dismay at their apparent betrayal. "What have you done?"

As the others began to clutch their bellies in pain, Kritten stuffed the other bottle of the cure in their pack and turned to flee. They sprinted straight for the passageway to the Overworld that Farnum had carved out, and they kept running up it as if the Ender Dragon itself was on their heels.

IF YOU BUILD IT . . .

To Farnum's delight, his friends had agreed to help him with building an obsidian portal on the zoo's grounds, despite any misgivings they might have had. He had to admit to himself that he was a bit nervous about it himself. The idea of creating a portal to the Nether right there where he worked and lived was unnerving, but he was ready to give it a shot.

Once he'd gotten the strider back to the zoo, everything had turned around for Farnum. He was on the way to building the place he'd always dreamed of but never done much to actually create. He wasn't about to back down from that now.

Despite the surprising and growing bravery that he'd displayed recently, Farnum nearly screamed when—late one night while the others had already left for the day—the piglin he'd met in the Nether showed up at the gates to his zoo. Okay, he had to admit to himself later, he had screamed, but only a little.

"What are you doing here?" he asked the piglin once he'd managed to recover from the shock. "How did you find me?"

The piglin—their name was Kritten, as they reminded him—

couldn't even understand Farnum, of course, much less answer him. Despite that, Kritten did their best to explain how and why they'd arrived at the zoo, using a complex and nearly incomprehensible series of gestures and meaningful grunts.

From what little Farnum could decipher, the piglin had come through the obsidian portal by which they'd met each other. How else would they have managed it, right? And then they must have followed him all the way back here.

Finding the tunnel he'd carved to the surface made some sense, but he was stunned that the piglin had managed to track him all the way back from there to the zoo. He wondered then if they had, in fact, done that or if they'd just wandered around aimlessly until they stumbled upon him.

Maybe they'd followed the strider here? The animal did have a distinct smell that Farnum found only slightly unpleasant, but it might have been enough for someone with a nose built like a piglin's to follow.

It made as much sense as anything else, which was to say *not much*.

Of course, how Kritten had gotten here wasn't nearly as important as why. What were they doing here? Why had they sought him out? What did they want from him?

These were simple questions with apparently complex answers that Kritten was unable to communicate with grunts, snorts, and squeals. Of course, it was impossible to tell if they understood what Farnum was asking them or if they were simply ignoring him and trying to tell their story. The most that Farnum got out of them was that the piglin had really wanted to find him, for whatever reason, and they were overjoyed that they'd actually made it happen.

It was around then that Farnum figured out why Kritten seemed to be in such a rush about it. The piglin started to turn a little green, and the rush of energy they'd been running on began to fade. The look on their face turned from excited to desperate.

Kritten took off their pack then and pulled out a glass bottle. They uncorked it, tipped it over their face, and tried to shake the last dregs inside it into their mouth.

They set the bottle down and stared at it in despair. Very little had come out of it, and they seemed like they badly needed whatever had once been in there.

"What was that?" Farnum asked. "How can I help?"

An idea struck him, and he guided Kritten over to the crafting table he had in the back of his quarters. The piglin thanked them for the effort with a kind nod but then turned the bottle upside down over the table to show that not only was it empty but that they didn't have the proper ingredients to fill it.

"What do you need?"

The piglin's coloration had gotten worse. Whatever they wanted, they weren't going to be able to ask for it with simple gestures.

Then they stuck a finger in the air as if they'd just gotten a fantastic idea. They reached into their pack again and found a stick of charcoal. They took it and began to draw something on the blank wall over the crafting table.

Farnum started to object to watching someone scrawl on his wall with a bit of charcoal, but he stopped himself and waited as patiently as he could for the piglin to finish. When they were done, they stepped back, flung their arms wide, and pointed both of them toward what they'd just drawn.

An obsidian portal.

"You want me to take you back to the obsidian portal?"

Kritten couldn't have understood their words, but they began snorting and nodding vigorously in agreement. What else could they have said, right?

Farnum swallowed hard. He had already told himself he'd never have to go back into the Underworld to find that portal, and now here was Kritten pleading with him to do exactly that.

"All right," he said, trying to get the overexcited Kritten to calm down for a moment. "I just need to get some things together—and see if I can get my friends to come with me."

He brought them to the table in his kitchen and sat them down there. "Wait here. I'll be right back."

With that, he ran off to gather his friends.

He ran as fast as he could, promising each of his friends that he would explain along the way. It didn't seem like it had taken him much time at all, but when he returned to his kitchen with Mycra and Grinchard in his wake, he found Kritten slumped over on the table.

Grinchard actually took a step back. "It's a piglin!"

Mycra rushed to the piglin's side. "Were they like this when you left?"

Grinchard stopped themself from reaching for their sword, but if Kritten hadn't been unconscious, Farnum had no doubt that the explorer would have drawn it.

"Didn't I mention that?" Farnum said by way of an apology, although he wasn't quite sure how it mattered.

Grinchard squinted at Kritten, making sure they weren't going to leap up and attack them all. "Piglins are dangerous. They usually just attack people on sight."

The explorer looked the others over. "Are either of you wearing anything gold? The greedy things see gold and they seem to lose all sense." Apparently satisfied that no one in the room was wearing anything that might trigger an attack, Grinchard crossed their arms over their chest and trained wary eyes on the suffering piglin.

Farnum opened his mouth to leap to Kritten's defense and then remembered how the piglin had attacked him when they'd first met. "Maybe it's all just a big misunderstanding. Or maybe they're not *all* bad. This one here is the one I met when I was in the Nether, and they were decent to me. Eventually."

Grinchard gave Farnum an *I'm impressed* look. "You did better with them than anyone I've ever heard about then. Lots of people who meet them for the first time never survive to tell anyone about it."

Farnum glared at his friend, exasperated. "Now, if that was the case, how would anyone know that?"

"You just find them full of piglin arrows."

Mycra prodded Kritten and shook their shoulders but didn't get any response. "Whatever their intentions, they don't look like much of a threat at the moment."

Grinchard peered into Kritten's face, pulled back their eyelids for a moment, and then stepped back. "Now *that's* out cold. They're still breathing, but not particularly well."

Farnum glanced around the kitchen. "What could have happened to them? Do you think they drank or ate something that didn't agree with them? Actually, they weren't looking all that good when I left."

"Piglins are allergic to our world," Grinchard said flatly. "They can't take it over here."

"What? Seriously?" Farnum found this hard to believe.

"That's why we don't have to worry about them following us over here. If you ever encounter a piglin in the Nether, all you have to do is run back through an obsidian portal, and you're in the clear. They don't even try to chase after you."

Grinchard cocked their head and stared at Kritten, mystified. "Well, not usually. The ones that are foolish enough to try it turn into zombified piglins not too long after. Anyhow, this one sure took their sweet time coming after you."

"They're not a threat. They helped me in the Nether. They gave me the strider!"

"And then all that time later managed to track you back here and collapse in your kitchen. Wild. Just wild."

Mycra rubbed the back of her head. "Maybe Grinchard's right. Maybe it's something to do with the Overworld that's making them like this."

Farnum pointed at the bottle Kritten had left on his crafting table. "They tried to drink something out of that, but it was all gone. Maybe it was some kind of medicine?"

"If it's all gone, it doesn't matter. That won't help us at all."

"Well, if we don't figure out some way to help this piglin, they're going to die on us. Right here."

"I have a solution," Grinchard said. "In fact, we already started on it."

The others stared at them, waiting for them to continue.

"We need to get them back to the Nether, right?"

"It's too far back to the gate," Farnum protested. "We'll never make it."

"How long would it take for us to finish the one that we started here?"

Everyone turned toward Mycra now. She looked flustered for a moment as she tried to figure out how to answer the question. "Not long," she finally said. "I don't know if it'll be soon enough for the piglin, but it could be worth a shot."

"Then let's do it," Farnum said. Kritten's breathing already seemed shallower than when they'd walked in and found them like this. "Now!"

LET'S MAKE A DEAL

The last thing Kritten remembered was sitting at the table in Farnum's kitchen and doing their level best to stay awake. The potion they'd drunk had finally worn off entirely, though, and they had no more defense left against the poisonous effects the Overworld had on their kind.

It seemed to them that the sickness was even worse on the surface than it had been in the cavern, but maybe that was just because they'd been exposed to it all for so long. They knew when they reached Farnum's house that they needed help fast. They just didn't know if they could make the Overworlder understand in time.

And then they woke up back in the Nether.

At first Kritten was terrified that they had somehow wound up back in the Great Bungus's bastion and were now awaiting execution at Uggub's hands. Then they saw Farnum and two other Overworlders leaning over them, and the advisor wasn't sure what to feel.

Relief, sure, at least about still being alive. They had no idea how long they'd been back in the Nether, but they felt perfectly fine now—and there wasn't another piglin in sight.

But what did this mean now? They hadn't really planned that far ahead. They'd only wanted to get away from Bungus and Uggub before they put an end to the advisor. It was hard to think too much about a future when you weren't sure you were going to have one at all.

Farnum reached out to help Kritten to their feet, and they accepted the assistance. As they glanced over the Overworlder's shoulder, they saw a brand-new obsidian portal right there, and they realized that Farnum had brought them into a whole different part of the Nether. Instead of the crimson forests that Kritten was used to, they found themselves standing in the middle of a wide expanse of netherrack spotted with rivers and lakes of lava that seemed to sprawl on forever under the relentlessly reddish roof.

They had to be in the Nether wastes. Kritten had rarely felt so exposed, and they instantly longed for the relative safety of a crimson forest. They had no idea how far they might be from Bungus's bastion.

Hopefully it was far enough.

One of the other things that Kritten had learned from deciphering the pictograms in that cave in which they'd first met Farnum was how obsidian portals worked. You just needed a lot of obsidian and a bit of fire to get it going.

The trouble, of course, was that there was no water in the Nether so it was impossible to make obsidian, and it didn't occur there naturally either. The only source of it would be from obsidian portals that had already been built—or had somehow been ruined—but even then Kritten figured you would need something to mine it with or you couldn't do anything with it. The advisor didn't have any such tools and had never seen them.

The fact that someone like Farnum and his friends—who clearly were not powerful figures in the Overworld—had managed to construct an obsidian portal gave Kritten an idea. If they could manage it, why couldn't someone as smart as the advisor give it a try?

Kritten used gestures to express their eternal gratitude to Farnum and his friends for saving their life. If the Overworlders hadn't gone to such extraordinary measures, the advisor would surely have died in Farnum's kitchen.

Farnum's friends hung back and allowed him to deal with the piglin, which pleased Kritten. It was hard enough to try to communicate with one Overworlder, much less three at a time. On top of that, none of the others seemed to trust Kritten much, although the advisor was used to that. In piglin society, no one trusted anyone anyhow.

After Kritten finished thanking Farnum, the Overworlder still seemed concerned about the advisor's health and safety. He pointed to his pack and then to theirs, asking if there was anything that Kritten might need from him and his friends.

Kritten made a show of not wanting to bother the Overworlders any further, but—as they had hoped—Farnum insisted. The advisor "reluctantly" decided to take him up on his offer. Now they only needed to figure out a way to communicate what they wanted to him.

Kritten pointed up at the obsidian gate, and Farnum nodded at them, apparently confirming that this was the way that they had brought the advisor back to the Nether. Kritten waved that all off, trying to make it clear that he had misunderstood what they had meant.

This time, Kritten pointed at the obsidian portal and mimed holding a pickaxe and chopping at the black rock that made up the frame of the portal. Realization dawned on Farnum's face as he understood what Kritten wanted—or so they hoped.

Farnum held up his hands to ask Kritten to wait while he conferred with his friends. The three of them moved away to be able to speak with one another without Kritten listening in, even though it would have been pointless for the advisor to try.

When Farnum explained to the others what Kritten wanted, they shook their heads, some harder than others. They weren't all that excited about giving Kritten anything and seemed to think they'd done enough for the piglin by saving their life.

While Kritten found it hard to argue with that kind of logic, that wasn't going to keep them safe from the piglins in the Great Bungus's bastion. And if they weren't going to give the advisor what they needed out of the goodness of their hearts—which Kritten had never really expected anyhow—then the advisor would have to offer them something they wanted in trade.

Kritten didn't know the other Overworlders at all, but having walked through Farnum's bastion—or whatever he called the place he lived in—they had identified what he wanted: animals and more of them.

Kritten drew a crude image of a strider on the ground, then beckoned Farnum over to see it. Despite the advisor's lack of artistic talent, Farnum immediately recognized what they had drawn and became excited. He pointed at it over and over and barked out some unintelligible words to his compatriots. This seemed to finally pique their interest too.

Then Farnum pointed to the drawing of the strider and tried out a number of different gestures until Kritten figured out what he meant. *More.* But not just more. *Different.*

Farnum wanted new creatures for the displays in his place. A new strider might be okay, but something different would be even better. And that was something that Kritten thought they could deliver.

The fact that the mobs they needed to capture might feel differently about that was a problem that the advisor would solve later. They hoped.

The advisor had no idea what might seem exotic and unusual to an Overworlder—the creatures of the Nether were all far too familiar to Kritten—but they were willing to keep bringing them creatures until Farnum got something he liked. All they wanted in return was obsidian and a diamond pickaxe with which to shape it.

The others gazed at Kritten with suspicion. Clearly they wanted to know why the advisor desired these things and what they proposed to do with them.

Explaining this without any common language was tricky, but what choice did Kritten have but to try?

The advisor tried to focus their attempts to communicate on the fact that having a way to access the Overworld from wherever they happened to be in the Nether would make them safe. Kritten could not be sure where the place they were at right then was, and using the first obsidian portal—the one through which Farnum had originally met them—was too dangerous. They wanted to be able to build another one close to where they lived.

Kritten did not, of course, share the fact that they had been exiled from their current home and that, from a certain point of view, any one place was probably as good as another. Glancing around the area, though, Kritten could see that this place—which was somewhere in the Nether wastes—was *not* safe to live in, and they hoped that the Overworlders would agree with the advisor on that salient point at least.

It seemed to take forever, but eventually Kritten and Farnum managed to get the other Overworlders to agree to their deal. Farnum would give Kritten a diamond pickaxe and the remaining obsidian that they had on hand, and Kritten would go out and find creatures to put on display in Farnum's exhibitions. On top of that, the advisor agreed to toss in plenty of netherrack to help make the mobs feel at home in the Overworld.

Farnum and Kritten even shook hands on the deal, which Kritten had once been told was a weird sign of deep respect between Overworlders. The piglins didn't care much for such things. With them, any bargain was only good for as long as both parties cared to keep it up. When that ended for either side, so did the agreement.

On the surface, the deal Kritten had struck with the Overworlders seemed like it would be good for everyone involved. The advisor didn't really understand why Farnum wanted animals— whether to show off to other Overworlders or as the subjects for experiments of his own—but if he was willing to hand over things that were incredibly valuable in the Nether, they weren't going to argue with him.

In fact, Kritten was already coming up with ideas for things that they could do with the ability to build an obsidian gate. Or— better yet—obsidian *gates*.

Once the Overworlders returned, they shut the obsidian portal down behind them. Kritten didn't blame them for that. They would have done the same.

After all, you never know what might come creeping out of the

Nether after you. It was one thing to leave an open portal at the bottom of a pit or in an abandoned cave that few people could ever reach. It was another thing entirely to leave that same passageway between worlds open in your home.

Of course, Kritten could have reactivated the obsidian portal at any point they wanted. Most creatures in the Nether wouldn't have any notion about how to manage that—which was perfect in the advisor's mind. That made them that much more valuable to others who might want to use the portals.

Others like the Great Bungus.

TRICKS AND TREATS

This time when Kritten entered the bastion, they went in through the front gates with their head held high. They informed the guards that they were here to see the Great Bungus, and they chuckled as they watched one of them scurry away to alert their leader to the fact that the advisor had returned.

Kritten had no doubt that the guard would also track down Uggub and let the brute know of the advisor's arrival as well. That didn't bother them in the least. They just signaled for the other guards to lead the way to the throne room.

By the time Kritten entered the throne room, Bungus and Uggub were already waiting for them, and they did not look pleased.

More to the point, Uggub seemed furious, steaming and ready to draw their axe and put an end to the advisor at a single nod from their leader. Bungus, on the other hand, seemed ready to listen, at least for a moment.

"Hail, the Great Bungus!" Kritten called out as they swept into the room. Normally they wouldn't stand on such ceremony with Bungus—they'd known each other far too long for that—but they felt like making an impression on everyone else in the room. The advisor hadn't shown up here to beg for their life. They were here to deal in earnest.

"Hail, Kritten!" the Great Bungus responded from his throne.

"Hail, nothing!" Uggub growled as they stalked toward the advisor. "You got a lot of nerve showing up here like this! How about I save us all some time and kill you now?"

"Then you would prove that you're just as much of a fool as everyone thinks!"

"You're right, I—! Wait, what?" Uggub couldn't believe that Kritten was standing up to them. Not so long ago the advisor had been Uggub's prisoner, and they had only escaped through trickery. To come back here as if nothing had happened at all was a massive insult to the brute.

Just as Kritten had intended.

Uggub drew their axe and brandished it at Kritten's head. "You can't trick me again! Not with your feet and not with your tongue!" If the two of them had been alone, Kritten knew that the brute would have cut them down right then and there.

But they weren't alone.

"Stop right there, Uggub!" The Great Bungus remained seated in their chair, showing the brute—and everyone else in the room—that they didn't even need to rise to put Uggub back in their proper place.

As Bungus intended, Uggub froze, their axe hefted halfway up in preparation for a vicious strike. The brute didn't look back at the leader for confirmation but simply stopped, waiting for their next orders.

Kritten allowed themself a smile that they knew would only make Uggub angrier. They had been ready to leap out of the way if the brute had actually taken a swing at them, but it pleased them no end to watch Uggub squirm under Bungus's gaze instead.

Bungus cut straight to the heart of the matter. They'd never been one for banter. "What is your grand plan, old friend?" The term dripped with sarcasm. "Given how you left us, it had better be a good one!"

"It doesn't matter!" Uggub bared their teeth at the advisor. "I'll put an end to you either way!"

Kritten laughed out loud. "Even you aren't that shortsighted! I understand if you want to kill me! But I only did what I had to in order to get away! None of you would have done any less!"

"None of us were about to be put to death!"

"I respect the Great Bungus and his flawless judgment!" Kritten wondered if they were laying it on too thick, but when it came to matters like this it was hard to overdo it. "And I'm sure that judgment will turn in my favor as soon as I can explain myself!"

"Words are cheap! Words are tricks! The time for words is done!"

Bungus snorted at that. They weren't about to let Uggub dictate what happened here. "Speak, advisor! Tell us what you came here to say!"

Uggub glanced back to glare at the leader, stunned that Bungus would give Kritten so much leeway. But other than acting offended, Uggub didn't do anything to stop it.

"I ran away because I needed to implement my plan!" Kritten spoke not just to Bungus but to anyone else in the bastion who might be listening in. The walls inside the place were terribly thin. "I have figured out the solution to all of your problems!"

Uggub scoffed at them. "Does it involve all of us putting our tails between our legs and running away like you did?"

"It involves us invading the Overworld!"

Kritten watched the guards in the corners drop their jaws in awe. Uggub shot the advisor through with a suspicious glare, but Bungus motioned for them to continue.

"You saw the pictures that line the inside of that cave in the Overworld, Great Bungus! They tell the saga of when an ancient piglin civilization stormed the Overworld and conquered the weaklings there with our crossbows and our axes—and all sorts of other fantastic weapons too, like this monstrous mace! Back in the days when our bastions were new and our people knew nothing but victory!"

The Great Bungus nodded at this as if they had both seen the images on the wall and understood them, which Kritten thought was unlikely. Bungus and Uggub had probably fled for the safety of the Nether shortly after Kritten had left them, but Bungus wasn't likely to admit that—or admit that they didn't understand the images. Especially not in front of everyone in the throne room.

"As proof that the tales told on that wall are true, I offer this ancient weapon, known as a *flail*." Kritten reached into their pack and drew out the amazing weapon they'd found in the cave and laid it at the Great Bungus's feet. Everyone in the room gasped at the flail, and Bungus snatched it up and began to swing it about, a mean grin forming on the ruler's face.

"So what?" said Uggub. "That was long ago, and we can't just walk into the Overworld whenever we want! Your little trick proved that!"

"Does the fact that you have returned to us prove that your

cure didn't work so well?" Bungus asked as he let the weapon's block smack into the ground next to him with a satisfying thud. "Otherwise, why would you come back?"

Kritten smiled. This was exactly the question they wanted to be asked. "Because I have concocted a grand new plan!"

Uggub rolled their eyes at this. "Just like you always do! And like always, it is only talk!"

Frustrated by the interruption, Bungus motioned for the brute to shut up. "What exactly do you mean?" they asked Kritten.

"My cure lasted much longer than I had hoped!"

"For how long?"

"If it was a permanent cure, they'd still be hiding out there!" Uggub snapped.

Kritten didn't let the fact that the brute was right slow them down. "Long enough for me to make it from that cave all the way up to a settlement in the Overworld!"

The Great Bungus scratched at their chin. "So we *could* invade the Overworld! All we need are crates full of that cure! Can you make that for us?"

Kritten bowed before the leader, showing them the proper deference. "I can, Great Bungus!"

Uggub grunted in disbelief. "This sounds like a trap to me! We bring our entire army up there, and then we run out of time! Even if we win that battle, we would lose the war!"

"This is true!" Kritten admitted, much to Uggub's shock. The brute narrowed their eyes at the advisor, fully expecting another trick.

They didn't know how right they were, but it was a *great* trick that Uggub couldn't possibly see coming. Kritten relished that thought for a moment before they continued.

"We would be stuck there, unable to return to the Nether in time! But I convinced the Overworlders to build another obsidian portal!"

It took a long moment for the others in the room to understand exactly what that meant. The Great Bungus was the quickest on the uptake.

They narrowed their eyes at the advisor. "You managed to speak with an Overworlder?"

Kritten nodded.

"And you could make sense of that nonsense they jabber?"

"Enough to trick them into making a portal right in the heart of their settlement."

Bungus nodded along as they puzzled out just what that meant. "So we can invade them, conquer them, and then return here before the Overworld poisons us?"

"Precisely!"

The Great Bungus clapped their hands together with glee. "Wonderful! Then we can do it! We can actually do it, just like they did in days of old! We can invade this strange place of theirs and make it our own! Soon the Overworld and all of its riches will be ours!"

"Ha!" Uggub snorted derisively. "What good is one little settlement to us? Are we then to live there and just wait for the creatures from some other settlement to rally to their cause and attack us?"

There had to be far more than a single settlement in the Overworld, Kritten knew, and once word of a piglin invasion reached those other places, the creatures there would not ignore the threat that an army of well-armed piglins would present. They would arrive in force to drive the piglins back into the Nether, which would leave them right where they'd started, only weaker and fewer in number.

"The *one settlement* will be but the first! That will be the beachhead from which we will conquer the whole Overworld!"

Uggub hefted their axe. They were getting tired of this argument and were ready to put a swift end to it. "And if we can only tolerate being there for not even a full day at a time, how will we manage that?"

"Because we don't have to stay in that same settlement forever! Instead we can strike at all of the Overworld settlements and destroy them one by one!"

Uggub scoffed at the thought. "And you think that they will wait patiently for us to do this?"

"They won't have a choice! We will take the battle to them!"

"From that one little settlement? Ha!" Uggub snorted so hard that they nearly lost their balance.

"No! We can strike at each of their settlements from the Nether through the obsidian gates!"

"Two gates are not enough! One in a settlement and one that comes out in a cave? They would never be enough!"

Kritten smiled at this. Now they had them. "Believe it or not, you fool, I agree! But I'm not talking about one portal or even two! I'm talking about having as many portals as we need! As many as we could possibly want!"

The Great Bungus actually stood up from their throne and leaned toward Kritten, more confused now than ever. "What is it that you are saying?"

"I am telling you that I have figured out how to build obsidian gates! And once we have enough obsidian, we can put new ones wherever we want!"

The head of Uggub's axe drooped and clanged to the floor. The urge to fight with Kritten—to kill them—had drained right out of them. In this room, at this moment, the advisor had utterly defeated them.

The Great Bungus, on the other hand, leaped down from their throne and charged straight at Kritten. When they met, the leader picked the advisor up into the air and swung them around. "You did it! I knew you would do it! I never doubted! I always knew!"

Kritten kept their mouth closed, not wanting to ruin the moment by pointing out that Bungus had entirely lost faith in them and exiled them from the bastion. If the advisor had been so rude as to mention this, the leader would have certainly claimed that they did this on purpose to encourage Kritten to come up with this exact solution, so this amazing result was actually the direct result of the way Bungus had treated them.

In a way, Kritten admitted, this was true. If they'd not been kicked out of the bastion—if they'd not been so desperate that they'd fled to Farnum's home to escape Uggub's wrath—they might never have figured out what they needed to do to allow the piglins to invade the Overworld.

But Kritten wasn't about to tell the Great Bungus that.

THE NEW ZOO

The deal that Farnum had made with Kritten had turned out even better than he could have possibly hoped. The two of them had met in the Nether several times since, and the animals that the piglin had brought for him had all been amazing.

Farnum didn't like to keep the obsidian portal open all the time, so he ignited it every evening to see if Kritten had brought him something new. If not, he shut it down and tried again the next day. Most days, Kritten wasn't there, but when they were Farnum always had plenty of obsidian ready to trade with them.

One of the first things Kritten had found for Farnum was a leucistic axolotl, just like the one he'd been chasing when they first met! In fact, he wasn't at all sure that it wasn't the exact same creature. The piglin could easily have gone back from the Nether into that cavern and captured it—assuming the rare axolotl had still been living there, of course.

But Kritten had brought him all kinds of other things too. The most intriguing of these so far was a creature called a hoglin. It looked a lot like a pig, but it had a fan of fur sticking up from its spine and a pair of tusks jutting from its mouth.

Also, it was a lot meaner. Farnum had taken care of pigs before. He'd even had them in his zoo. But he had a hard time getting the hoglin to stop attacking him, even though he'd lined the enclosures for all the Nether mobs with netherrack to help them feel more at home.

Fortunately, he and his friends had been prepared for this. Grinchard had reminded Farnum that all sorts of dangerous creatures lived in the Nether, so they should be prepared if Kritten brought one of them to the zoo. To that end, they'd built a number of reinforced habitats that could keep even the meanest creatures captive.

After all, Farnum couldn't have such vicious beasts breaking loose and terrorizing the town. If that happened, they'd have to kill the offending creature, and to Farnum that was entirely opposite of the whole point of having a zoo. The place was meant to show people all sorts of amazing animals—and to keep them safe from the people and the people safe from them.

The first time Kritten brought a hoglin through from the Nether, Farnum was as excited as he could be. The creature fired his imagination and set him to wondering how many different kinds of stunning beasts they might be able to introduce to the zoo.

Unfortunately, the hoglin didn't do well in the Overworld. While the strider had been perfectly fine once it got warmed up, the hoglin reacted to the world much more like a piglin did—like it had been poisoned. Farnum supposed he should have spotted that before Kritten had left the mob with him, but he'd been too excited at the moment to notice.

Farnum had wanted to hustle the hoglin back to the Nether before it became too sick, but the beast attacked him any time he got close to it. He wasn't able to get close enough to it to pick it up and hustle it away before it died.

That had been sad enough for Farnum. He'd fallen to his knees and cried over the poor animal, which hadn't done anything to deserve such a horrible fate. And then the dead animal stood up and attacked him again.

The transformation from hoglin to zoglin—a zombified hoglin—shook Farnum so hard that he almost didn't escape. The zoglin took a large bite out of his leg as he was climbing out of its pen, and he had to have Mycra patch him up.

While Farnum lay there on the other side of the fence, injured and watching the zoglin throwing itself against the fence as it kept trying to get to him with undead ferocity, he said, "Maybe this isn't the kind of animal that belongs in a zoo."

Grinchard laughed at that, trying to put their friend at ease. "Are you kidding? It's perfect. It's already dead, so you don't have to worry about killing it! And you don't have to feed it anything either!"

"Just make sure it doesn't take *another* bite out of you," Mycra said as she bound Farnum's wound.

Farnum was just glad that Mycra was talking to him. They'd had a bit of an argument over her diamond pickaxe, and that had led to her avoiding him a lot of the time.

To be fair, it was less an argument and more Farnum pleading for Mycra to give up her diamond pickaxe and her saying no.

"It's mine," she said. "Not yours. Mine. And I need it for my job."

"Can't you just make another one? They don't seem all that complicated."

Mycra scoffed at him. "Making one is easy enough. Finding the materials you need to make one is the tricky part. Diamonds are rare and expensive. A pickaxe like that is even rarer."

Farnum had known that when he'd cut the deal with Kritten, but he'd figured that he could talk Mycra into seeing it his way. So far he'd not had any luck on that count.

"But I need it for the zoo! I promised Kritten I'd get them one."

"Just keep giving them the obsidian, which they want so badly—although for who knows what reason. You have a ready source for that right here in the zoo, and they seem happy enough with it."

"Eventually they're going to get tired of all that and want a diamond pickaxe. Why not just trade them one right now?"

Mycra rolled her eyes at him. "For one, it's not yours. For two, you should hold out a bit. They just started bringing you animals. You really want to give them everything and then just hope they keep coming back with new creatures for you?"

"I trust them. We made a deal."

Mycra gave Farnum a sad shake of her head. "That's sweet. I suppose that's one of the reasons I like you so much, but you really shouldn't trust people you don't know that well."

"Yet!" Farnum added. "I don't know them that well *yet*. But we're getting to know each other better all the time. And so far they've held up their end of the bargain. I just want to make sure I can hold up mine too."

"Then you better start saving up for a diamond pickaxe of your own to give to them."

That had put an end to the conversation then, but Farnum was always looking for an excuse to restart it. He just didn't want to do so while Mycra was taking care of his leg.

For the meantime, Kritten seemed to be fine with accepting as much obsidian as Farnum could make for them, and they continued to bring him all sorts of new animals. After the incident with the zoglin, Kritten had shown up with a fresh hoglin—hostile but still alive at least.

"I don't think I can accept this one," Farnum said. "It's not that I don't want to have such a wonderful creature in my zoo, but I just don't want another one of them to die on me. If I can't take proper care of it, I'd rather it went free."

That explanation was more for his friends who were listening to him than for Kritten, who couldn't understand a word of it. When the piglin gave him a confused grunt he pointed at the new hoglin and then over at the zoglin and gave Kritten an emphatic shake of his head.

The piglin understood this and disappeared back into the Nether with the hoglin. The next day, though, Kritten returned with the same hoglin in tow and with a chest filled with old bottles. When they presented the hoglin to Farnum, Kritten uncorked one of the bottles, which was filled with an odd liquid that smelled like old dust.

Then Kritten fed the contents of the bottle to the hoglin, which slurped it up in an instant. Afterward, Kritten hung around for several minutes to observe the hoglin, and the creature seemed absolutely fine. Clearly delighted, Kritten offered both the hoglin and the bottle to Farnum with a humongous smile.

"I just have to feed it some of this?" Farnum held the bottle up in front of him. Kritten nodded vigorously.

Farnum tried to ask the piglin how often he needed to give the hoglin the medicine, but he couldn't work out a way to manage it. He wondered if time in the Nether ran differently than it did in the Overworld, but he supposed it didn't really matter. He and his friends would just have to keep an eye on the hoglin and give it the medicine whenever it started to look like it was feeling ill. They'd figure out a schedule for it eventually.

Most of the other animals that Kritten brought to the zoo, thankfully, didn't require as much maintenance. The only trouble was building enclosures for them fast enough to accommodate them all, but Mycra and Grinchard pitched in with that. Farnum knew that he wouldn't have been able to manage such incredible expansion without them.

One night, while the three of them were relaxing after a long day's work, Farnum offered up a toast. "I just want to thank you all for everything you've done for me and my zoo. Without you, I'd probably be collapsed somewhere under a feeding trough."

"Or maybe the zoglin would still be feeding on you!" Grinchard cracked.

Farnum's leg had healed just fine, but the memory of that had stuck with him. It served as an object lesson that you couldn't be too careful around wild animals — especially ones from the Nether.

"Yet another reason you all deserve my thanks!"

"It's all in our best interest," Mycra said. "If you got turned into a zombie yourself, I'm sure you'd be trying to eat us forever!"

"It's okay, though," Grinchard said. "We'd be sure to put you in one of the zoo's cages too and watch after you for all eternity."

Farnum cackled at that. "I always said the zoo is my life! I just wasn't planning on it being my death too!"

Later that evening, Farnum and the others gathered near the obsidian portal in the back of the zoo so that he could ignite it like he normally did. It activated just like usual, with a field of purple swirling all through it.

When Kritten had something to trade, they often bounded right through at that point, hauling something wriggling with them that would bring a huge smile to Farnum's face. This time, nothing appeared, at least not at first.

Mycra clapped Farnum on the back. "We'll try again tomorrow."

"It's been a while." Farnum gazed at the portal, worried. "Do you think anything might have happened to Kritten?"

"Well, it can't be easy trying to gather all those beasties for the zoo," Grinchard said. "Maybe they caught the wrong end of one of them?"

Mycra scoffed. "That's a horrible thing to say. Now he's going to worry all night." She turned to Farnum. "I'm sure they're fine. They're probably just looking for something really special for you now. They've already brought you all the easy animals. It takes a while to get the tougher ones, I'm sure."

Farnum sucked at his teeth. He wasn't sure what to do. He couldn't really go hunting for Kritten in the Nether. It was far too dangerous to be there for long, and anyhow, that was the deal he'd made with the piglin. They provided the animals, and he provided the obsidian.

He'd just have to wait until tomorrow. "If we don't hear from them soon, we'll have to go in and have a look around for them," he said. "But not tonight." The others nodded in solemn agreement.

Just as Farnum was about to give up entirely and shut down the obsidian portal for the night, the purple field flickered.

Farnum's hopes rose like a rocket. He couldn't wait to see what Kritten had brought for him this time.

But it wasn't Kritten who came through the portal. Instead, it was the biggest piglin he had ever seen, and a legion of well-armed piglins followed in the massive brute's wake.

WANTON DESTRUCTION

"It's a whole army of piglins!" Grinchard shouted at the top of their lungs as they drew their sword and steeled themself for battle. "We need to shut that portal down now!"

Mycra drew her sword too and was ready to fight. Farnum cursed himself for not bothering to bring his own blade along that night. He'd come to trust Kritten, so he was never armed when he went to meet with them. He'd always figured if something went wrong during one of their trading sessions, he and the others would just chase the diminutive piglin back through the obsidian portal and shut it down behind them—permanently if necessary.

He had never imagined that any other piglins would come snorting and snarling through the portal instead of Kritten—nor that they would be twice the little piglin's size!

"It's too late!" Mycra shouted as she backed away from the horde of piglins rushing through the portal. "There are too many of them already!"

Farnum hoped that his friend was wrong, but he didn't see

how. A dozen large and ferocious piglin warriors had already stormed into the zoo and were blocking off any approach to the obsidian gate. They seemed to be daring Farnum and his friends to give it a shot anyhow so they could cut any such foolhardy souls down.

The first of those would be Grinchard. "We have to try, or we'll never have another chance!"

Of them all, Grinchard was the best with a sword. When they dove into the mass of piglins, swinging their blade left and right, the brutes gave way before them. Heartened by Grinchard's success, Mycra leaped into the fray after them, weaving her sword about herself to form a shield that none of the piglins dared charge.

Weaponless, Farnum stood back and shouted his encouragement to the others. He admired the way they burst into action with less than a moment's notice and were already pushing the piglin invaders back. "You got them! Go, go, go!"

As Farnum's friends drew closer to the obsidian portal, the flow of piglins stopped, and it looked like that might be all of them. Hope soared in Farnum's chest—and then came crashing right back down into the dirt.

The rush of piglins had only slowed, it turned out, to let an even bigger piglin stomp through the portal. They seemed to be so large that they barely fit through the portal, and Farnum's cheers strangled in his throat the moment he saw them.

The massive piglin held a large flail in their hand—the biggest Farnum had ever seen—and when they brought the business end of it slamming down into the ground, Farnum could feel the earth shake. Then the gigantic piglin let loose a roaring snort that chilled Farnum's blood.

"It's a trap!" he shouted at his friends. "Run!"

Despite the obvious danger, Grinchard refused to retreat in the face of the piglin onslaught. Instead, they forced their way through the smaller piglins until they came face-to-face with the brutal giant who had just forced their way through the portal.

To their credit, Mycra followed in Grinchard's wake, never hesitating to make sure they kept the other piglins off the explorer's back. The piglins gave way before her, swinging their blades at her but not offering much in the way of challenge.

At least that was so right up until Grinchard came up against the massive piglin standing between them and the obsidian portal. The moment that happened, the towering brute held up their mighty weapon and let loose an even louder snort than before, and the piglins closed in around the zoo's defenders like a vise.

The big piglin—*biglin?* Farnum thought, his mind always trying to classify the things he encountered—brought that massive flail down on top of Grinchard. The explorer might have dodged out of the way, but smaller piglins had them pinned in on both sides. The best they could do was hold up their sword to try to parry the incoming blow.

Grinchard did just that, holding the weapon's hilt with one hand and the end of the blade with the other, bracing themself behind it as best they could. The golden flail's head came hurtling down like a meteor arcing out of the sky, though, and snapped the blade in two.

"No!" Farnum shouted, which did as much good as anyone could have expected.

The impact knocked Grinchard flat on their back, and they disappeared under a horde of piglins swarming over them.

Mycra leaped forward then, laying all about with her own

blade and trying to drive the piglins off Grinchard's fallen form, but other piglins leaped between them, separating and surrounding each of them.

That was the moment that Farnum knew it was all over for them. His friends were some of the best and most experienced fighters he'd ever met, but even they couldn't stand against so many foes. They were outnumbered and overpowered and flat-out doomed.

"Stop!" he shouted at the top of his lungs. "Stop it! We give up! We surrender!"

He wondered if his friends would consider him a coward or— worse yet—a traitor for trying to stop the fight like that. He didn't know or care at that point. He just wanted them to survive.

Even if he'd had a sword of his own—and somehow knew how to use it better than any of his friends—he couldn't have done a thing to turn the tide. It would have been like battling an ocean with a spoon.

The piglin leader—if that's what the gigantic one was— snorted at Farnum's cries, but they didn't do a thing to stop the other piglins from utterly overwhelming the others. Grinchard and Mycra disappeared beneath the waves of piglins that hauled them down beneath the surface of them as if to drown them.

"Stop it!" Farnum shouted. "Stop it!"

The piglins ignored his cries, and Farnum wondered if his friends had already been killed. He charged forward a few steps, still yelling at the piglins to stop, but the ones in the back turned around then and brandished their weapons at him.

Farnum realized then that this problem was much bigger than just his friends or his zoo. This many piglins could destroy the entire town. He had to warn everyone.

He spun on his heels and sprinted for the zoo's front gates, shouting the entire way. "The piglins are invading! Help! The piglins are invading!"

When Farnum got to the front gate, he realized he'd shut and locked it when he'd closed the zoo that evening. As he reached out to undo the lock, the first of the piglins behind him caught up with him and bonked him with the hilt of their axe.

Farnum spun around and fell to the ground. He couldn't see anything but angry piglins coming at him, and he thought this was the end. "Mercy!" he shouted as he flung his arms over his head. "Mercy!"

BETRAYAL!

By the time Kritten strode through the obsidian portal and into Farnum's zoo, the initial assault was over. The Great Bungus had given Uggub the honor of being the first through the portal and leading the attack against the Overworld. Then he had come through himself, after the vanguard of the best piglin fighters had joined Uggub on the other side.

Kritten spent the entire time making sure that each of the piglins heading off for the battle first drank an entire bottle of the potion that the advisor had whipped up to protect them from the illness the Overworld would otherwise inflict upon them. They had taken the time to craft chests full of the stuff, and those sat in a stack right next to another stack of chests filled with the obsidian Farnum had traded with them.

The piglins guzzled down the whole first chest full of potions quickly, and Kritten had been forced to open a second chest just to make sure that every one of them was properly protected. The potion wouldn't last forever, though, so the advisor had hustled every one of them through the portal as soon as they'd chugged down their full dose. The fighters needed to make the most of the time that they had.

Once the last of the now-protected piglin warriors dashed into the Overworld, Kritten closed up the second chest of potions and followed right after them.

Privately, Kritten had hoped that Bungus's warriors wouldn't kill Farnum and his friends. The Overworlders had been kind enough to Kritten during all their trading sessions, and it seemed like a shame that such useful trading partners might pay for that with their lives.

Kritten knew better than to try to appeal to Bungus's kindness. The brutal leader didn't have any, which is partly how they'd managed to ascend to their current position as leader of a bastion. Instead, the advisor had pointed out that they'd made great strides in learning to communicate with Farnum and that Farnum could serve as a perfect guide for them as they explored the Overworld. Killing the zookeeper would only slow that process down.

Bungus had grudgingly seen the wisdom in that and ordered their warriors to spare Farnum's life. The trouble, of course, was that to the piglins one Overworlder looked pretty much like another. Only Kritten could really tell them apart.

Bungus couldn't depend on those aggressive battlers to make a distinction among their opponents during their initial assault, so instead the order went out that the Overworlders inside the zoo would all be spared.

"How are we supposed to do that?" Uggub had wanted to know. "When we hit them, they need to go down! We can't have them running off to warn anyone!"

Bungus had smacked Uggub across the snout for being the kind of fool who would dare to question the leader's orders. "Bring them down as fast as you can! Once they're down, haul them to me!"

Uggub had glared at Bungus as they stood back up to answer the piglin leader. "We might wind up killing them anyhow!"

Bungus had raged so hard at this insolence that Uggub had flinched away. "So they get killed! This is war, and Overworlders are going to die! But if you kill these ones, you will be next!"

That had seemed to settle the argument, but Kritten still worried that the piglins would *accidentally* kill Farnum or one of his friends. It was just too easy to make that kind of mistake when you were attacking someone with a weapon, and the piglins who followed Bungus tended to be prone to such errors.

So Kritten was relieved—and perhaps a little surprised—when they saw that Farnum and his friends had been tossed into one of the still-empty animal enclosures, one that the advisor had yet to fill with a new creature they were supposed to bring there from the Nether. That opened up all sorts of possibilities for them that would otherwise have been cut off permanently.

Farnum seemed like he'd been watching Kritten from the moment they'd arrived in the Overworld. When he saw the advisor glancing in his direction, he waved at them, trying to get their attention. Rather than ignoring him entirely—which had been Kritten's first impulse—they gave him a firm nod of recognition and dismissal. They would talk to him eventually, but they had other things to deal with at the moment.

Kritten looked around the zoo and saw that the piglins had massed at the zoo's front gate, rattling their weapons with anticipation. Uggub stood at the entrance, blocking the others from leaving quite yet, while the Great Bungus loomed over them.

Bungus barked out orders to the piglins, instructing them as to how they would overwhelm and defeat the settlement. Following the advice Kritten had often given in the past, Bungus kept the orders short and sweet. That made those directions hard to misinterpret and mess up, although Kritten knew that some of the piglin warriors would figure out brand-new ways to screw things up that would surprise them all.

"This is just the first battle in our new war!" The Great Bungus's voice was so loud that Kritten figured any Overworlders in the neighboring buildings must have already heard the shouts. If so, they would be ready for the piglins when they stormed out of the place, but it was too late to do anything about that.

"From here, we will loot settlement after settlement! Land after land! Soon all the riches of the Overworld will be ours! And no one will be able to stop us!"

The piglins let out a raucous cheer in unison, and the Great Bungus bared all their teeth at them in approval. Kritten figured that anyone in the settlement who didn't already know the piglins were there must be aware of it now.

Not that knowing about their doom would prevent it.

The Great Bungus pointed toward Uggub at the gates and shouted louder than ever over the cheering. "Now unleash the piglins of war, and let the Overworld tremble in fear!"

At that cue, Uggub threw open the gates to the zoo and stepped aside as the piglin warriors charged out into the settlement like a swollen river breaking through the floodgates. The noise grew to a deafening crescendo for a moment and then drifted off into the settlement proper like rolling thunder.

"Well done!" Kritten said as they marched up to the Great Bungus to congratulate him for a flawless operation so far. "We should have this town looted to the walls in no time!"

Uggub scoffed at them. "We? You should not include yourself in that number, traitor!"

"Traitor?" Kritten glared at the much bigger piglin. "If not for me, none of you would be able to stay here long enough to loot a single building, much less the whole place!"

Uggub loomed over Kritten, reminding the advisor that the brute could stomp them flat with their bare feet. "Serving the Great Bungus out of fear is not loyalty! It is cowardice!"

"Says the piglin who led a surprise attack against weakling Overworlders! Who is the real coward here?"

"Enough!" the Great Bungus boomed. "We have triumphed today by working together! Together we can loot the whole of the Overworld! Or I can put an end to you both here and now for arguing with each other and then go loot this place by myself!"

Both Uggub and Kritten allowed Bungus's outburst to cow them. Neither of them was about to apologize to the other for speaking plainly about how they actually felt, but they were wise enough to shut their mouths for now—at least while Bungus was watching over them.

"Now, allow me to enjoy our pillaging in peace!" The Great Bungus strode out of the zoo after their rampaging piglins to the sounds of the clash of weapons and the cries of the fallen, a massive smile curving below their chunky snout.

Uggub and Kritten watched their leader swagger off into the night-shrouded settlement, looking for doors to bash in and homes to loot. Soon enough Bungus spotted something that looked like their kind of fun and lumbered off toward it, the head of their golden flail spinning high over their head and an earsplitting snort rising from their throat.

Uggub turned to Kritten and glowered at them. "Stay here, traitor! The glory of a battle like this is not for the likes of you!"

Kritten knew that the smart thing to do would have been to allow Uggub to have the last word before charging into the battle—but they couldn't resist needling the brute one last time. "If it wasn't for me, it wouldn't be for the likes of you either!"

Uggub had been halfway through the gate when Kritten spoke, and they stopped dead there and spun around. "What did you say?"

Again, Kritten was sure that the wise course of action would have been to apologize there—or at least to pretend that they'd said something entirely different. Instead, they doubled down on the insult. "You heard me! Or is there nothing but muscle between your ears? Maybe that's one of the side-effects of *my cure!*"

Uggub stepped forward and backhanded Kritten to the ground in the blink of an eye. As the advisor waited for the stars to clear from their eyes, the brute growled down at them. "You had better learn your place! The Great Bungus may be in charge of me, but I am in charge of everyone else! Defy me, and you will pay for it!"

Kritten shook their head to clear it. "You need me!"

Uggub chortled at the advisor's bravado. "Bah! We need your cure, yes, but you?"

Kritten leaped to their feet. "No one else knows how to make it!"

"That's a problem I can solve myself—by beating the secret out of you!"

"You wouldn't dare!" The moment the words left their lips, Kritten knew they were wrong. Uggub would not just dare to wrench the formula for the cure out of them, they would enjoy doing it.

"Why not?" Uggub said. "Who is going to stop me?"

"If you hurt me, the Great Bungus will make you pay!"

Uggub chortled at their desperation. "Bungus is not your friend! Not anymore! Who do you think ordered me to get the cure from you?"

Kritten's eyes grew wide in fear, and they looked for someplace safe to run. Uggub stood between them and the gates, but maybe they could make it to Farnum's kitchen and from there out a back door.

Just as Kritten's feet started to move, though, Uggub's arm lashed out, and the brute caught the advisor by the scruff of their neck. From there, the brute hauled the hapless advisor up into the air, leaving their legs churning uselessly below them.

"Put me down!" Kritten screeched.

Uggub snorted at them. "Oh, I'll put you down, all right! Just not here!"

With that, Uggub carried Kritten at arm's length all the way to the pens in the back of the zoo. When the brute reached the one in which the piglins had imprisoned Farnum and his friends, they grabbed hold of Kritten with one hand on their neck and the other on the seat of their pants and hurled them over the top of the fence.

Pain shot through Kritten when they landed inside the enclosure, and they howled out in agony and curled up into a ball.

"Now stay there until this battle is over! There will be time to finish with you later! I'm not going to miss out on all this looting!"

Uggub turned and stormed off, viciously laughing out loud until long after they disappeared through the zoo's front gate.

Once the pain started to subside, Kritten got to their knees and crawled their way to the enclosure's fencing. It ran so high over their head that they were stunned that Uggub had actually managed to toss them over it. There didn't seem to be any way to climb over the bars or to squeeze between them. In short, they were trapped and trapped good.

As Kritten tried to figure out how to solve this brand-new problem, someone cleared their throat behind them. The advisor turned around to see Farnum standing right there.

STRANGE BEDFELLOWS

Farnum had never imagined that someone might use the enclosures in his zoo to imprison him and his friends. When they had built these environments, they had concentrated both on making them excellent habitats for their guests and on ensuring that those guests could not escape. The last thing they needed was something like a wild zoglin on the loose again.

Now that diligence was working against them. The piglins who had invaded the zoo and handily defeated them had tossed them in here, locked them up, and walked away with the keys — which they'd taken from Farnum's belt.

Fortunately, the piglins had left the rest of the animals alone, including even the zoglin. All of the animals were safe in their pens and would be just fine — at least until their next feeding.

Farnum's first concern at that point had been to make sure that his friends were all still breathing. Grinchard had gotten the worst of it and was still unconscious. Mycra seemed mostly all right, although it had taken Farnum a while to revive her.

"Those invaders crushed the air out of my lungs," she said when she finally woke up. "When I passed out from it, I thought I was gone for sure."

"I'm so sorry." It took everything Farnum had not to dissolve into tears. "This is all my fault."

"Don't be silly," Mycra said as she tested herself for broken ribs. "It's not your fault. Blame the piglins. Speaking of which, have you seen your piglin pal throughout all of this?"

Farnum shook his head.

"Then it might not even be their fault either. We don't know, and assigning blame doesn't help us right now anyhow. Our first priority is taking care of each other, so you made a good start there. Let's see how Grinchard is doing."

Working together, Mycra and Farnum managed to get Grinchard stable. The explorer was still too weak to stand, much less throw themself back into the fight as they wanted to, but they were also grateful to be alive.

"You need time and rest," Mycra told the Grinchard. "That'll give you the best chance to recover."

The explorer was too beat to argue with her, even if they wanted to.

As Mycra finished up with Grinchard, Farnum spotted Kritten coming through the obsidian portal. By that time, he had started to worry about them, as it seemed like the flow of piglins coming through from the Nether had already stopped entirely without Kritten joining them. Had they been captured and tortured? Even killed?

When Kritten strode through the portal, though, snorting like they were on a mission, Farnum's feelings for them turned from worry to fury. Not only was Kritten unhurt, they looked proud of all the damage the other piglins had inflicted upon the zoo.

Farnum leaped to his feet and waved at Kritten, determined to demand an explanation from them. He saw them look right at him—they even nodded at him—and then ignore him and continue on their way. They didn't even slow down!

"Don't worry about them," Mycra said. "Shouting at them won't do you any good. It's better if they and the rest of the piglins continue to ignore us."

"We can't just let them get away with this. They're going to attack the rest of the town!"

"And there's nothing we can do about it from here. The whole town has to have heard all the commotion from these piglins arriving already. They'll be as prepared as they can be."

Farnum fumed at Kritten's betrayal—and partly at how pragmatic Mycra could be about everything. He wanted to do something—anything—to save the town. He was the one who'd built the obsidian portal that had allowed the piglins to invade, and he felt responsible for it.

It did not escape him that he'd built it to save Kritten's life, and that the piglin—whom he'd come to think of as a friend—had used it to betray him. If he'd never done that—if he'd never moved here, never started a zoo—everyone would be fine. The town would be intact, and Grinchard wouldn't be hurt.

It was all his fault. He had to do something to fix it. Anything!

"We need to figure out a way out of here," Farnum insisted.

"I have some ideas about that," Mycra said as they sat down next to Grinchard. The miner wasn't moving all that well either, and Farnum worried that she was pushing herself too hard on his behalf. "But you're not going to like them."

Farnum wanted to argue with her, but the gigantic piglin

leader—who seemed to be named Fungus, as best Farnum could make out—was giving a terribly loud and obnoxious speech at the gates. The cheers from the rest of the piglins drowned everything else out, so Farnum decided to just shut up for the moment and watch them.

Farnum gasped in horror when the piglins charged out of the zoo to launch their assault on the rest of the town. He worried for all of his neighbors' lives and homes. Even if they survived, he wondered how they could ever forgive him for opening a portal that these monstrous invaders could storm through.

Once all the other piglins had left, though, Kritten fell to arguing with a gigantic piglin brute, and the little traitor apparently lost the grunting match, as they wound up being thrown into the same pen with Farnum and his friends.

Farnum's first instinct was to run over and kick Kritten in the ribs. If he couldn't take out his guilt and frustration on Fungus and the rest of the piglins, then Kritten would have to do.

Before he could, though, Mycra put a hand on Farnum's arm to ask him to wait for a moment, and he complied with her wishes. His own judgment had turned out to be terribly suspect so far that day, so he was content to rely on hers.

As Kritten dusted themself off, Mycra released Farnum's arm. The zookeeper walked up behind Kritten, who was still crumpled in a pile on the ground. When his patience evaporated, which didn't take long, he cleared his throat to alert the piglin to his presence, and Kritten raised their eyes to face him.

Then the little piglin rose to their knees in front of him and began to snuffle and weep. After a moment, they stopped, seemingly astonished at their own tears, as if they'd never seen such a thing before. And then they went back to weeping again.

At first Farnum was entirely unmoved. He was too angry about the piglin invasion to even think about forgiving anyone associated with it.

Then he realized that, as far as his fellow townsfolk were concerned, he would fall firmly into that category of responsibility himself, and he felt his heart soften just a bit.

Farnum had always been bad at holding a grudge. He'd tried it a couple times in the past, but it always wound up seeming like it was more trouble than it was worth, as the grudges often bothered him far more than they did the people he tried to hold them against.

Besides, the fact that Kritten had been thrown into the enclosure with Farnum and his friends served as a pretty good indication of Kritten's position among the piglins.

Maybe the little traitor had been betrayed too? That made Farnum feel a bit better, and he realized that it also meant that there wasn't any reason that he shouldn't work with Kritten now—at least to escape the enclosure.

Farnum knelt down next to the piglin and helped them to their feet. They wiped the tears from their face as they stood in front of him, and their expression transformed from dismay to determination.

"Farnum," the piglin said to him with a warm snort.

The zookeeper wasn't ready to put their betrayal behind him yet. "Kritten," he said in a much colder tone.

The piglin pointed at the gates to the zoo and made squeals and gestures that Farnum could only interpret as Kritten saying they needed to get out of the pen, fast. He couldn't help but agree, but he wasn't sure he could trust his own judgment any longer. After all, his trust of Kritten had endangered the entire town and gotten his friends beaten badly.

He looked over at his pals. Grinchard had fallen unconscious, which was probably for the best. Mycra, though, was watching him, and she looked at Kritten and then gave Farnum a solemn nod.

"That piglin pal of yours might be a traitor, but they have nothing to lose by working with us at this point." Mycra's voice was weaker than Farnum would have liked, but that didn't detract a bit from her point. "You can't take on all those piglins yourself—and Grinchard and I aren't really in any kind of shape to help you."

Farnum shook his head, still hesitant. "But how can I trust them?"

Mycra chuckled, which turned into a painful cough. "You can't. But you know that now. That should make working with them easier, right? They can't shatter your illusions about them a second time."

That was the wisest thing Farnum had heard all day. He turned back to Kritten and gave the piglin a hard stare. "All right." He stuck out his hand. "Let's do whatever we can to take those invaders down. Partners?"

He pointed to himself and then to Kritten and back. "Partners."

Kritten took Farnum's hand and shook it, grunting something that Farnum charitably interpreted as, "Partners."

GET THE OBSIDIAN

Kritten's entire body was sore, but at least they didn't feel so alone anymore. When Uggub had decided to drop the facade of tolerance and thrown the advisor into that animal cage with the Overworlders that they'd already defeated, Kritten had been relieved. They had feared that Uggub was going to kill them on the spot rather than save them for some horrible torture they planned to inflict in the future.

As long as Kritten was alive, they had a chance. Being imprisoned in a cage wasn't great, but it was better than dying.

The first thing they did was throw themself at Farnum's feet and beg for mercy. If they'd been in his position, they would have felt justified to put an end to someone who had betrayed them so badly, and Kritten needed to eliminate that possibility straightaway, one way or the other.

Once again, to their surprise, they remained breathing.

Kritten could hardly believe that Farnum had been foolish enough to forgive them—or at least put aside his hard feelings long enough to work with them—but they weren't going to let that go to waste. No piglin would have given them a second chance like that, and they needed to make the most of it.

Within moments, Kritten concocted a plan to foil the piglin invasion of the Overworld, but the trouble was that they needed to communicate this somehow to Farnum, and they only had a few words they knew how to use with each other. Gestures would have to do most of the heavy lifting in their explanations.

It wasn't that Kritten was against looting the Overworld. If they were in charge, they'd have launched a similar campaign of pillaging. But they weren't in charge, and that was something that they now realized needed to change. Working as Bungus's advisor had only gotten them banished and then thrown in a pen.

If Kritten wanted to stop living under Bungus's rule—or, worse yet, Uggub's—then they were going to have to take charge of the clan themself. It was the only way.

They weren't quite sure how they were going to manage it, but they knew that it started with them getting out of this pen and then spoiling all the looting—which made Farnum and his friends the perfect allies. For now.

Kritten put up their hands and mimed chopping away at something with a pickaxe. At first Farnum had no idea what they were trying to say, but his friend—the one called Mycra—figured it out. They needed a pickaxe or some other kind of tool if they were to get out of there. That wasn't all, of course, but it was a solid start.

Farnum seemed to remember something, and he raced off to a far corner of the pen to find it. A moment later, he held a battered iron shovel over his head in triumph, as if he had just uncovered the greatest treasure of all time.

Kritten found it hard to argue with Farnum's enthusiasm, but they had to bring him back down to earth. The shovel he'd produced would be fine for digging their way out of the enclosure, but it wouldn't be enough for what they really had to do.

For that, they'd need a diamond pickaxe.

That had been the main reason that Kritten had bargained so hard with Farnum for such a tool. They had known that such a powerful tool might be vital to them at one point or another. They just hadn't dreamed that it would be in a situation like this.

But when you wanted to work with obsidian, there was no better tool.

To get Farnum to understand this, Kritten pointed at the shovel and nodded. Then they walked over to a part of the enclosure where they could see the obsidian portal and stabbed their finger at that as well.

Farnum furrowed his brow at the advisor and shook his head. He didn't quite understand what they meant. He pointed at the edge of the pen and hefted the shovel, indicating that he could dig their way out of there with it. He just wasn't thinking far enough ahead of that yet.

Kritten ran their hands over their face and tried again. Farnum was sharper than Uggub or Bungus, for sure, but it was frustrating to have to work with him like this. They should have spent more time learning how to talk with each other instead of concentrating on just getting what they wanted out of each other and moving on. Mentally Kritten put that at the top of their list of things to do—once all this was over.

Kritten kept pointing from the shovel to the obsidian portal over and over again until Farnum finally figured it out. He leaped up in excitement once he knew what they wanted, and he hooted his triumph at Mycra.

Then his face fell. He knew what Kritten needed, but he didn't have the right tool at hand. He turned to Mycra and asked her if she could help. It sounded to Kritten like she said something positive, but when she gestured off toward Farnum's living space, Kritten frowned too.

Mycra had been the only one of the Overworlders whom Kritten had seen with a diamond pickaxe. (They'd coveted it from that moment and always kept an eye peeled for an opportunity to swipe it, although the chance had never come.) Mycra must have left that wonderful tool in Farnum's place, perhaps in the kitchen. Either way, it was far out of reach.

Upon reflection, Kritten supposed that had been an excellent stroke of luck. If Mycra had been carrying the diamond pickaxe when the piglins had crushed her, they would no doubt have taken it from her. Bungus or—worse yet—Uggub would be charging around the settlement with it right now.

Since she had left it in Farnum's quarters instead, that meant it was still someplace safe—at least for now. They needed to get out of the pen and grab it before the rest of the piglins returned and decided to loot every corner of the zoo too.

Farnum asked Kritten a question then, and they didn't understand a word of it. He pointed at the shovel and then at the obsidian portal and shrugged, a confused look on his face. *Why?*

Kritten nodded at him to show that they recognized his confusion. They mimed knocking down the obsidian portal with a pickaxe. Then the advisor pointed at themself—and at their snout in particular—and pretended to start choking on the Overworld's poisonous air, finally collapsing in a heap.

Ah! That Farnum understood. If they could destroy the obsidian gate, they'd cut the piglins off from their supply of the potion that protected them here—and eventually the protection would wear off. It would take some time, but the piglin problem would take care of itself.

Maybe that would put Kritten in a similarly bad situation, but they knew something no one else did: how to make more of the cure. With any luck at all, they'd be able to leverage that to their advantage. The best they could do now was cause as much chaos as possible and then play the angles better than the idiots currently in charge of their people.

That was something Kritten felt good about betting on.

Farnum motioned that they should get started right away then, but Kritten hadn't quite filled him in on the whole of their plan. He needed to know the rest of it, or he might blow the whole thing for them.

It wasn't enough to just destroy the obsidian portal. They had to destroy all the obsidian they had here as well.

Kritten cast about for a bit, trying to spot the place where the piglins had stored the chests of obsidian that they'd brought back into the zoo with them from the Nether. When they did, they jumped up and down and pointed at it until Farnum came over and saw exactly what they were so excited about. Once he did, Kritten then mimed using a pickaxe on that stuff as well.

This seemed to confuse Farnum more than just about anything that they'd tried to discuss so far. They wanted him to destroy the rest of the obsidian. Otherwise, the Great Bungus would simply repair the broken obsidian portal with that fresh material. Or maybe even just build an entirely new one from scratch.

They had to take care of all that obsidian first. Otherwise, destroying the working portal wouldn't mean a thing. It would only slow the piglins down a bit, and that wouldn't be nearly enough to defeat them.

Farnum just wasn't getting it, though. Maybe it was because Kritten was pretending to use a pickaxe on the obsidian, which wouldn't really destroy it, would it? It would simply mine the material, breaking it down a bit further but not actually getting rid of it.

They needed to do something that did much more than breaking the obsidian down from big chunks into smaller chunks. They needed to get rid of it entirely.

Could they move it back into the Nether before they broke the obsidian portal? That might work, but there was a *lot* of obsidian there. Carrying the obsidian through the portal one chest at a time would take forever.

They'd have to come up with a different way, although Kritten didn't know what it might be. While they knew a lot about the Nether and had learned a great deal about the Overworld, the only thing they knew about obsidian was that it was extremely tough material and that you could build these amazing interdimensional portals out of it.

The advisor had never mined actual obsidian. They'd only hauled away what Farnum had been able to produce for them every time they'd made a trade. They'd never even built an obsidian gate with it—not yet. They had come to the Overworld with great plans for such construction, of course, but that had all fallen apart almost immediately.

Kritten wondered how the Great Bungus thought they would continue with their conquest of the Overworld without the advisor—if they actually were in on the betrayal of Kritten, as Uggub had said. While Kritten might not know everything there was to learn about obsidian, the rest of the piglins knew even less.

Uggub had claimed that they would beat the secret of the cure out of Kritten. It wouldn't be any more trouble for them to knock what they knew about obsidian portals out of their head at the same time.

That was probably the only reason Uggub hadn't killed Kritten on the spot. Somewhere in that tiny, violent brain of theirs they must have realized that they needed the advisor, at least until they could get the information they required out of them.

At this point, Kritten threw up their hands and snorted in despair. They crumpled to the ground, sat on their haunches, and stared off into the distance.

They couldn't come up with the solution to this problem on their own. They didn't know enough to make it happen.

Farnum came over to stand next to Kritten then and put his hand on their shoulder in a way that—much to their surprise— brought them comfort. The advisor looked up into the Overworlder's eyes and saw clarity there.

Maybe Kritten didn't know what to do from that point, but Farnum seemed like he did. The advisor was going to have to trust that he could figure it all out from the point at which Kritten had left off.

They didn't have any other choice.

And that scared them most of all.

TIME TO DIG IN

Farnum could barely believe what he'd learned from his wordless conversation with Kritten. While they couldn't understand each other's languages, it turned out that the time they'd spent together making deals had put them on a similar wavelength. They could get a lot more from gestures, grunts, and meaningful expressions than he would have expected.

"Kritten wants to destroy the obsidian portal," he said aloud, to Mycra if nobody else. "That will trap the piglins in the Overworld."

"Is that really such a good thing?" Mycra wanted to know. "I mean, I'd much rather we trapped them in the Nether instead."

Farnum gave her an amused grunt. "If you can figure out a way to have them file peacefully back through the portal before we destroy it, I'd be delighted to hear it."

Mycra barked a bitter laugh. "But we can't destroy the obsidian portal until we destroy all of the obsidian floating around here first. Right?"

"Right. Otherwise, they'll just repair or rebuild the gate, and we're right back where we started."

Mycra raised a feeble hand, as if she were a young child in class. "So if we destroy the gate, they'll be trapped here. And they'll get sick like Kritten did when they first got here, right?"

"That's the theory. And I guess that assumes they didn't bring gallons of the cure for that sickness along." He eyed the chests the piglins had hauled in with them, unsure what was really in them.

"Either way, what's to stop them from killing us all before they fall over and die?"

Farnum scratched his chin as he pondered that. "That's a good question. We should probably make sure we're somewhere else when that happens—if at all possible."

"Seeing as how Grinchard isn't in any condition to flee with us, that's going to be a neat trick."

"If you have a better—"

"I don't. Of course I don't. But that doesn't mean we shouldn't do it anyhow. Even if they kill us all . . ." Mycra trailed off and gazed at Grinchard, not quite ready to finish that thought.

"At least we'll have stopped them. Their reign of terror will end here."

"Exactly." Mycra gave him a weak smile. "So, how are you going to pull all this off, then? You need to get out of this pen first, right?"

"And then go find your diamond pickaxe."

"And then destroy the obsidian."

"And then destroy the gate. Probably in that order." Farnum tried putting on a brave face that he wasn't sure would convince anyone, much less someone he'd known as long as Mycra. "Simple, right?"

She coughed, her lungs still laboring to work properly. "You'd better get going then."

"Wish me luck."

She did so with a nod, and he left her there, hoping he would see her and Grinchard again. He walked over to the edge of the enclosure, hefting the iron shovel in his hands. He'd lined much of the floor of the enclosure with stone to keep the animals from trying to dig their way out, but they didn't have access to tools like this.

He also hadn't quite finished with this enclosure, which was why no creatures were already in here when the piglins tossed them into it. There were still a few spots where the floor was lined with netherrack instead of stone. The battered little shovel would probably get through that just fine.

He held up the shovel and readied himself to get started, but he found himself hesitating. Despite having mined his way out of the cavern in which the waterfall had left him, the idea of digging his way through the Underworld (as he continued to think of it) still terrified him.

He'd forged his way out of that cavern only because there had been no other choice. It had been a matter of dig or die.

And he'd had the strider with him then, a creature he'd felt responsible for and couldn't just abandon. This time instead he was with a piglin who'd already betrayed him once.

Kritten came up beside him and grunted at the ground in front of him, then to the shovel and then to the ground again. They clearly couldn't understand what he was waiting for.

He knew he had to do this. It was going to be hard and terrifying and awful, and he was going to hate every second of it. But he still had to do it.

He held the shovel before himself for a moment and then started digging. The dirt before him gave way easily enough, and he breathed a sigh of relief.

At that moment, voices grew nearer at the zoo's gates, and a platoon of piglins burst squealing back into the place.

Farnum froze for an instant, unsure of what to do. Mycra knew, though. "Keep going!" she shouted at him in a stage whisper from where she lay in the back of the enclosure. "Once you're underground, plug the hole back up! They'll never know!"

Unsure if he was doing the right thing and still scared of being caught, Farnum followed Mycra's orders. He dug down into the netherrrack as fast as he could, listening to the hoots and hollers of the piglin warriors echoing throughout the zoo above him.

Kritten followed him down into the hole and stood next to him. He still wasn't sure that he wanted the piglin with him. It was one thing to shake hands with them and another entirely to be trapped in a tight underground tunnel with them.

As the grunting above grew closer, Farnum heard a deep grunt calling out over all of their unintelligible babble. It was the voice of the big piglin who'd been the first through the portal—the one who'd thrown Kritten into the enclosure—and it sounded like they were snorting out orders to the others.

Farnum couldn't make out much of what that piglin was saying, but he made out the name Kritten. If they came looking for the little piglin and discovered they were missing—along with Farnum—they would be sure to tear the place apart looking for them.

He had to make sure they couldn't find them.

Farnum filled in the hole that he'd just dug, sealing both himself and Kritten into the Underworld and plunging the two of them into complete darkness. For a moment, Farnum froze, unsure where to dig or what to do. It was hard enough to dig a way through the Underworld, but doing so blind seemed utterly foolhardy.

Then Kritten lit a torch, and things seemed better.

The piglins had taken everything from Farnum before throwing him into the enclosure, but apparently Uggub hadn't been quite so careful with Kritten, having just tossed them and everything they were carrying into the pen. The little piglin might not have a weapon of their own handy—at least Farnum didn't see one—but the torch was far more valuable to them then anyhow.

The light steadied Farnum and gave him hope. Now, at least, he could see what he was doing—if not where he was going.

Still, he knew the zoo better than any other part of the Overworld. He'd been over every bit of it himself countless times and had personally built most of the structures inside of it. If anyone could figure out how to get to where the obsidian was being stored, it was him.

He dug down a little deeper first, afraid that the piglins might otherwise hear him tunneling through the ground beneath them. Then he headed off in the direction of the obsidian stores that Kritten had pointed out to him.

The stockpile sat just on the edge of the strider's enclosure, and Farnum felt pretty confident that he could judge the distance to there. He'd paced back and forth between that pen and this empty one over and over while he'd been building the enclosure. Of course, then he'd been able to walk freely rather than having to dig his way through the Underworld, so he wasn't quite as sure as he would have liked.

He would just have to do his best.

Even if they wound up in the strider's pen, that wouldn't be so bad. The strider was such a kind animal that Farnum had never put a lock on the cage to its pen. If it somehow managed to get out—which happened sometimes—it always stuck close, and the visitors to the zoo loved being able to meet it up close and pet it.

Of course, if they wound up coming up from the Underworld beneath one of the piglins that would be much worse. Much as he might wish it, though, Farnum didn't have any real control over that. He couldn't see where the piglins were now, any more than they could see him. He just had to trust that they wouldn't be wherever he and Kritten emerged.

The going under the zoo wasn't all that bad. Although the iron shovel wasn't Mycra's prized diamond pickaxe, it was good enough for mining through the Underworld beneath the zoo, although when he ran into the odd stone formation he had to dig his way around it. Despite that, Farnum tried to go slowly and methodically. He didn't want to run into any surprises like a vein of lava or an unceremonious drop into a deep cavern.

When he thought he'd gone far enough, Farnum stopped to rest for a moment. He looked to Kritten, who had followed behind him the whole way, illuminating the new tunnel with their torch, and pointed at the ceiling and shrugged. Did this look like a good spot?

Kritten seemed to understand what he meant, but that didn't mean they had a good answer for him. They gave him a shrug even more helpless than his own. He admitted to himself that his guess was probably far better than the piglin's would be. He wasn't sure why he'd bothered to ask for a second opinion—other than that he was frightened by the possibilities of what might happen next.

Despite that, he started digging upward. As he grew closer to the surface, he slowed, again not wanting to alert anyone above to his presence. If he was lucky, he'd emerge near the obsidian, and then he and Kritten could figure out what they were going to do with it.

Maybe they could simply ferry it underground and bury it where the piglins would have a hard time finding it? He wasn't sure that would be enough. If the choices for them were find the obsidian or die, they'd dig up the entire zoo hunting for it—and probably succeed.

As he reached the surface, Farnum stopped digging for a moment to listen through the thin layer of earth above him. He could still hear piglins snorting at one another all over the place, just as urgently as before, but he didn't understand anything they were saying. At least he didn't hear any of them bellowing out orders anymore.

Farnum raised the shovel and removed the last layer of netherrack standing between himself and the Overworld. Light from the zoo poured in from above, along with a rush of fresh air. Farnum allowed a sense of relief to wash over him with all that.

Then a long arm reached into the hole in which he was standing, grabbed him by the back of his neck, and hauled him bodily out of his tunnel.

Farnum screamed in terror as he was lifted into the air. For a wild moment, he was disoriented and had no idea what was happening to him. He was just going along on the most awful ride of his life.

When he finally came to a stop, Farnum found himself gazing into the eyes of the biggest piglin he had ever seen, snorting their hot and humid breath directly into his face. It was the one who'd come through the portal after most of the others, swinging his golden flail and sending the rest of the piglins off to ravage the entire town.

He'd been captured by Fungus.

THE BIG FIGHT

Coming face-to-face with Fungus—or whatever the gigantic piglin leader's name was—sent Farnum into an utter panic. He had no idea what to do or how to get loose, but he had a shovel in his hands, so he started swinging it.

The piglin leader had been snortling in Farnum's face till that point, close enough that Farnum could see the creature's saliva glistening on their tusks. Fungus must have seen that Farnum and Kritten had disappeared from the enclosure in which they'd been tossed and gone looking for them. Maybe they'd set guards at every one of the places they wanted to protect. Maybe Fungus had personally chosen to keep an eye on the obsidian, knowing just how vital it was to their plans for their invasion of the Overworld.

Or maybe they'd just gotten lucky. Either way, they seemed awfully pleased with themself, right up until Farnum slashed with his shovel at Fungus's arm.

Squealing in pain, the gigantic piglin let go of Farnum then but also flung him away, ensuring that he wouldn't just drop back into the ground where the piglins would have a hard time extracting him—and where Kritten had to still be hiding. Instead, Farnum went tumbling across the zoo's open floor and eventually came to rest against the gate of the strider's pen.

The animal nuzzled up against Farnum then, as happy to see him as ever and hoping for a treat. Farnum wished that he'd been in a position to reward the strider at that point, but it took everything he had to push himself to his feet instead.

Fungus—which honestly seemed like a terrible name for such a terrifying creature, although perhaps it referred to the scent of the piglin leader's breath—turned toward Farnum and let out a bellow of blind rage that curdled Farnum's blood. It seemed like the noise alone shook the whole of the world, but maybe that was just because it set Farnum trembling so hard.

Desperate to escape, Farnum spun around and opened the gate he'd landed against. It came open easily, and he shoved his way in, right past the strider, and ran.

Fungus lumbered after him and stood there in the gateway for a moment, surveying the strider's enclosure. To Farnum's great dismay, there was no way out of the place. He and his friends had built a tall and solid fence all the way around it, and a pool of molten lava lined its back wall.

The only way out would be for Farnum to start digging, but he knew that would take too long. The moment he started, Fungus would just rush over and grab him before he could get away.

Still, he had to do something—try something—*anything*.

That was when he saw the strider coming at him, and a plan came to mind. It was a ridiculous and probably pointless plan, but if he was lucky it would buy him enough time to come up with a better one. And at least it would be something other than waiting for the Great Fungus to storm in and brain him.

Farnum whistled for the strider to hustle over to him, patting his thigh to keep its attention. The animal trotted right over, and without missing a beat, Farnum leaped up onto its back.

Fortunately, Grinchard had left their saddle on the creature's back, and Farnum could slip right into it. The explorer had also been experimenting with leading the strider around with a warped fungus dangling from the end of a fishing rod, and he'd left those atop the strider as well, probably to the creature's frustration.

Unfortunately, Farnum hadn't practiced riding the strider much before, and he almost fell off the creature's other side. It took everything he had to hold on, and he dropped the shovel he'd been carrying in the process.

When Fungus saw Farnum jump atop the strider, they clearly knew that some sort of trick was coming, and they charged straight for the zookeeper as he tried to find a solid seat and a firm grip on the strider. The gigantic piglin's snorting roar frightened the strider, and it took off as if someone had jabbed it in the rear with a sword.

As challenging as this made it for Farnum to find that grip he was searching for, this turned out to be a good thing, as it kept both him and the strider out of the reach of Fungus's savage flail, which crashed into the ground behind them.

Farnum was still struggling to right himself atop the strider when it sprinted straight into the pool of lava in the back of its pen. Under most circumstances, this might have stopped Farnum's heart, but in this case he'd been planning to guide the strider back to the pool anyhow. This only served to impress upon him how imperative it was that he not let go.

The strider hauled up to a halt when it reached the back of the enclosure, standing right on the far edge of the pool of lava, exactly where Farnum wanted it. With the animal not moving for a moment, he was able to right himself atop it and get a firm grip on it so he could snatch up the fishing rod and warped fungus.

As he did, he looked back across the lava to see Fungus standing there on the edge of the pool, glowering at him and the strider. The gigantic piglin reached out with their massive flail, testing the distance from themself to Farnum. Although the zookeeper could feel the powerful breeze that Fungus's swings generated, the head of the flail itself wound up well shy of him, much to his relief.

Farnum resisted the urge to stick out his tongue at Fungus and taunt the piglin leader. While he might be safe from taking a direct blow from that awful flail at the moment, that didn't mean that they couldn't throw the flail at Farnum instead. It would only take a glancing blow to knock him off the strider—or to knock the strider over—and he would be incinerated immediately.

It was hot enough for Farnum sitting on the strider's back. He couldn't imagine how the animal could withstand contact with the molten rock, but it just strolled around on it all the time like it was nothing. In fact, it preferred to hang out on the lava, which kept it far warmer than any other part of its enclosure could manage.

Any other creature that Farnum knew of would be burned to a crisp in an instant—and apparently that included Fungus. The piglin boss roared at Farnum from the edge of the lava pool and snorted all sorts of things that were surely so horrible that the zookeeper for once felt glad that he couldn't understand the piglin tongue. He just hoped that Kritten could protect their ears.

As Fungus berated Farnum, some of the braver piglins came up from behind to cheer their leader on and mock the trapped zookeeper's plight. A few of them carried crossbows, which sent a shiver of fear through Farnum. As soon as they started firing arrows at him, he'd have to start moving. The lava wouldn't offer him any protection from their shots.

Furious as Fungus was, though, the moment one of the piglins bumped up against them, the leader reached down, grabbed the gloating creature, and hurled them at Farnum. The horrified zookeeper hunkered down and clung to the strider as tightly as he could, and the animal leaped aside from the incoming piglin. The poor warrior burst into flames as they landed and was reduced to ashes in an instant.

The rest of the piglins gave Fungus a wide berth after that, keeping well clear of their leader's reach. The huge piglin roared again in frustration, but now none of the others rallied to their side to egg them on.

Infuriated by the lack of support from their underlings, Fungus raised their golden flail over their head. Knowing what was coming next, Farnum whipped the warped fungus out right in front of the strider's nose, spurring it into action.

The head of the flail and its chain came spinning at them in a flat circle and just barely missed them. It was close enough to muss up Farnum's hair as it skimmed over his head. It crashed into the far wall, knocking a hole in it before it tumbled into the lava and began to burn.

Unfortunately, the hole in the wall was too far away for Farnum to reach it, and he wasn't sure that he could wriggle through it to get away anyhow. If he tried to leap for it and missed, he would certainly pay for his mistake with his life.

Instead, he guided the strider back to the spot in the pool of lava that was farthest away from the outraged Fungus and listened to the leader rail against them once more. The rest of the piglins edged even farther away from their ruler's ridiculous fury, terrified of becoming entangled in it.

Just as it seemed like Fungus might finally calm down—which meant that they would really become dangerous to Farnum and the strider—their second-in-command came up behind them: the one called Uggub.

Fungus didn't even notice Uggub at first. They were too engrossed with cursing Farnum and coming up with new ways to berate him. Fungus finally did hear Uggub chortling as they approached from behind, though, and the leader turned at the last second to chew out whomever had been brave enough to get within their reach.

That probably saved Fungus's life, but it wasn't enough to stop Uggub from laying into the leader with a cowardly attack.

Uggub slammed into Fungus from behind, but because the leader had started to turn, it was only a glancing blow. Even that was enough to knock Fungus off balance, though, and send them staggering toward the lava pit.

The leader stuck out one foot to steady themself, and it landed in the lava. Flames instantly shot up from the molten rock, setting the leader's leg ablaze.

Rather than falling into the lava, though, Fungus managed to shove themself away on their burning leg, and they tumbled backward onto the stones lining the deadly pool. Their leg had been ruined, but they managed to knock the flames out by rolling around on the ground before curling up into a tight ball and bellowing in excruciating pain.

Uggub stood over the injured Fungus then, raised their fist into the air, and snorted something that Farnum thought might have translated as "Now I am the Great Uggub!"

The rest of the piglins hesitated for the briefest of moments before they raised their weapons into the air as well and began to grunt in unison, "Uggub! Uggub! Uggub!"

THE GREAT UGGUB

From the moment the Great Bungus dragged Farnum out of his tunnel, Kritten had not known what to do. Part of them wanted to crawl out of the hole, follow Bungus, and demand that they leave Farnum alone, but the advisor knew exactly how well that would go.

Another part of them wanted to race back through the tunnel that Farnum had just dug and see if they could scrabble their way back into the pen in which Farnum's injured friends were being held. Maybe the advisor could pretend that they had been in the pen the whole time, waiting for the Great Bungus to come and set things straight after Uggub had tossed Kritten in there—which Bungus would surely see had been a mistake.

The most cowardly part of Kritten thought it might be best to just remain there in the tunnel, maybe a little bit farther back, and hope that no one ever came in after them. Then, when things had calmed down a bit, they might be able to sneak up into the zoo and maybe even slip through the obsidian portal and back into the Nether where they belonged.

No matter what, though, Kritten had long ago learned the hard way never to interfere with the Great Bungus when they were enraged, so the advisor waited a bit to see what happened to Farnum. If Bungus killed the zookeeper quickly, that would probably put the leader into a good mood.

If they decided to play with Farnum a bit beforehand—or maybe just tossed them back into the pen after beating them senseless—Kritten might be able to talk Bungus into showing mercy. But that would have to be later.

Despite their fear of discovery, Kritten's curiosity had gotten the better of them. They poked their head up out of the hole and saw that Farnum had done a far better job of guessing how far to dig than the advisor could have hoped. The chests of obsidian sat right there next to them, scant feet away.

When Farnum managed to leap on the strider and escape, Kritten couldn't help but silently cheer for them, even if they knew that this would probably mean a violent and painful end for them. When they managed to evade both a piglin and Bungus's massive flail hurled at them, the advisor couldn't believe their eyes. They had never seen anyone evade the Great Bungus's wrath for so long.

And then Uggub ambushed Bungus from out of nowhere.

Kritten had long suspected that Uggub would do their best to get rid of Bungus at the first opportunity. That was the piglin way: to take power from those who had it.

The trouble for Uggub was that Bungus was bigger and stronger than them, and it didn't seem like Bungus had lost any of their cunning or ferocity over the years that they'd been in charge of their bastion. Some piglins would have been content to wait for age to weaken such a leader, for the years to humble them in the way that other piglins could not.

But Uggub had never been all that patient. They had been looking for their chance to put an end to Bungus for years, and now that they had found it they were going to take it.

Uggub was a coward—the kind who would attack their leader without warning and from behind—but Kritten knew that the other piglins would never hold that against them. With Bungus out of the way, Uggub would take charge, and none of the other piglins were anywhere close to tough or large or devious enough to challenge them about it.

Kritten had worked with Bungus for so long—had advised them since they were young—that they weren't prepared to see them fall. Mentally they knew it would happen someday. In fact, they had decided that they might have to take action to make that happen themself. But emotionally they didn't know how to deal with it.

Something inside of them broke when they saw Uggub knock Bungus into that lava pool. When they watched the leader's leg go up in flames. When Bungus rolled back onto the pool's shore, the remains of their limb still smoldering.

Dismay overtook Kritten at that point and threatened to swallow them whole. They found themself emerging from the hole next to the obsidian without even realizing that their legs were moving. They simply pushed them up and out and forward.

At first, Kritten thought that they were moving toward Bungus, their longtime leader, their oldest friend. While the piglin leader had brutalized them for years, they had at least understood each other, depended on each other. Sure, Bungus had banished the advisor from the bastion, but that hadn't stuck for long, and Kritten had honestly never expected it to.

Kritten knew, though, that life for them under Uggub would

be like most piglins' lives: brutal and short. The traitor had no affection for the advisor. Uggub would kill them and replace them with someone far duller—if they replaced them at all. Many piglin leaders refused to rely on advisors of any kind, thinking that listening to someone else's opinion made them look weak, in a job in which weakness invited aggression.

That was why, when Kritten realized that their legs weren't carrying them toward Bungus but Uggub, they weren't surprised at all. The day of Bungus might be over, but the day of Uggub hadn't quite begun.

Not if Kritten could help it.

Kritten drew the blade that they always carried with them—the one that they'd kept hidden from Farnum and even from Uggub when the brute had tossed them into the pen—and they marched straight up to the traitor.

Uggub didn't even notice Kritten approaching. They were too busy gloating over their betrayal of Bungus and basking in the glory of having claimed leadership over the piglin warriors.

The other piglins, for their part, were too busy cheering for Uggub. It hadn't taken them long to recognize that Bungus was finished and Uggub would be in charge now. To make sure that their new leader didn't take them out too, they each made sure to cheer as loudly and obviously as they could.

They probably all thought that Kritten was doing the same thing. Perhaps the advisor was marching up to prostrate themself before Uggub and beg for mercy, which everyone knew they would never get. The best that the advisor to a disgraced leader could hope for was a quick death.

Kritten had higher hopes than that, but they depended entirely on Farnum stepping up and helping them out. The advisor hoped that the zookeeper would figure that out fast, or they would both be doomed for sure—and the entire settlement along with them.

Kritten kept their knife close to their chest, right up until they reached Uggub. Then, instead of kneeling in front of the celebrating brute, they hauled the knife up in both of their hands and brought it down hard, point first, right into the top of Uggub's foot.

The blade stabbed straight through the brute's foot until it struck stone below it.

The look of triumph on Uggub's face instantly transformed to one of agony. As Kritten hauled back on their blade, Uggub drew back their foot and began to hop away on their uninjured limb, howling in pain.

For a long moment, the rest of the piglins had no idea what had happened. Uggub had looked so strong and in charge. To see the brute already injured and wailing shook their faith in Uggub's ability to lead their people, and they instinctively recoiled.

Kritten did not waste any time. While Uggub hopped away from them, they pursued the brute with their knife, looking for another opening for a fresh attack. The advisor also shouted out, "Farnum!" plus one of the few other Overworlder words that they thought they understood, probably because they'd heard Farnum muttering it to himself while he'd been confronting his fears: "Dig!"

Farnum had been gawking at Kritten till that point, marveling at the advisor's bravery—or so Kritten hoped. Kritten could see how someone their size taking on someone Uggub's size would impress an Overworlder, but if the zookeeper didn't get moving right away, the act would turn out to be one not of bravery but of stupidity.

To their great delight, Kritten saw Farnum get the strider moving again, using some kind of strange contraption that dangled something in front of it. The animal launched forward, carrying the zookeeper from the relative safety of the lava pool and sprinting right toward the enclosure's wide-open gate. When the strider reached the gate, Farnum leaned over and scooped up the iron shovel that he'd dropped there when the Great Bungus had flung him away.

Farnum kept moving then, not even bothering to slow down. Kritten would have watched where they were going, but they already had their hands full with Uggub.

After the initial shock from the attack had worn off, the brute had put their injured foot back on the ground and focused all their pain and rage toward the advisor. Every step on the foot caused them horrible agony, which they expressed with a furious snort that made Kritten shudder in fear.

"You are going to die!" Uggub bellowed at the advisor as they lumbered in their direction. "I am going to break you into tiny pieces and smash every bit of you flat!"

Kritten did the only thing that they could do under such circumstances. They turned and fled.

With Uggub injured, Kritten thought they might actually have a chance to outrun the brute. Normally it wouldn't have been much of a contest at all. The brute's legs were longer and faster than the advisor's, and Uggub would have caught Kritten in a matter of a few strides.

Unfortunately, the rest of the piglins saw that as well and leaped to give their most likely new leader a hand.

Under other circumstances, most piglins would have stayed back and let the new leader establish their dominance by destroying their attacker. A few of them had started after Farnum, though, and now found themselves standing between Kritten and the gate the advisor was charging toward. They spun around and brandished their axes and crossbows at the advisor, more in self-defense than anything else.

When Kritten saw this, they peeled off to the side to avoid a direct confrontation with the piglins in the gateway. This, however, kept them inside the pen, which gave Uggub a much better chance of catching them. If they wanted to keep out of the brute's grasp, they were going to have to move sharp and fast.

Uggub roared at the others. "Don't you dare let that little traitor leave! I'll kill anyone who does!"

The rest of the piglins got the hint and joined in corralling Kritten away from the gate and toward Uggub. None of them would attack Kritten directly. To do so would have been to cheat Uggub of their chance for revenge on the advisor, which would incur not the brute's gratitude but their wrath. So they kept their distance from Kritten but made it clear that if the advisor came near them they would force them back into the center of the pen.

While Kritten didn't appreciate being forced into closer quarters with Uggub, they immediately saw how they could work this to their advantage. If Farnum figured out what the advisor wanted him to do, then Kritten didn't need to defeat Uggub—which was all but impossible anyhow. They just needed to keep from being killed long enough for Farnum to complete his mission.

"Go ahead, coward!" Uggub snorted at Kritten. "Run all you want! Wear yourself out! You're going to get tired before I stop being angry! And then you're going to die!"

THE PIT AND THE OBSIDIAN

Farnum had just about given up hope that he might survive the night when Kritten emerged from the tunnel that he'd dug. After the piglin's earlier betrayal, he had assumed that he couldn't count on any help from that quarter, so it heartened him to see them climb out of the hole and then *not* run in the other direction.

Then, as Kritten and Uggub began to fight, Kritten had squealed something at him—something that none of the other piglins would have been likely to understand: "Farnum! Dig!"

As Kritten said that, they'd pointed from the lava pool to the hole that they'd emerged from. No! To the stockpile of obsidian the piglins had brought with them from the Nether!

Farnum wasn't entirely clear on what Kritten was telling him, but thinking back on how he and his friends had made the obsidian helped him figure it out. Using water to cool lava produced obsidian, but you had to be careful about how you extracted the obsidian after that. If you weren't careful, the obsidian would fall back into the lava, which would melt it and destroy it.

Farnum was literally riding on top of a source of lava. If he could somehow dump the obsidian in it, he could destroy it all, but he didn't see a good way to do that. There were too many piglins standing between the chests of obsidian and the lava pool—including Uggub, who would kill him the moment they got the chance.

Kritten hadn't told him to bring the obsidian to the lava though. They'd squealed, "Dig!"

Farnum hadn't understood that at first. It wasn't like he could dig through the lava. That would kill him instantly.

But he could dig through the Underworld, from the spot where the obsidian stockpile was, right to the lava pool. If he couldn't bring the obsidian to the lava, he could bring the lava to the obsidian instead!

Of course, trying to do this while Uggub and the rest of the piglin invaders stomped around overhead would be a challenge. The only thing that gave him a bit of hope was how Kritten was keeping Uggub busy. The little piglin wouldn't be able to keep away from the brute forever, so Farnum would have to move fast.

The moment Farnum reached the hole next to the obsidian stockpile, he leaped off the back of the strider and dove into it. Then he set to work with his shovel.

The first thing he did was dig out the space directly beneath the stockpile, as he knew he'd need a place for the lava to flow into. He considered collapsing the entire stockpile into the pit he'd dug, but he decided against it, as he didn't want to raise the suspicions of Uggub and the other piglin warriors yet.

With that done, Farnum poked his head back up over the surface to see how Kritten was faring against Uggub.

It did not look good.

The brute had gotten their hands on Kritten and had hauled them high into the air to choke the life out of the little piglin, who was kicking their feet out like mad in a vain effort to hurt Uggub's arms. The rest of the piglins had gathered around Uggub to cheer their efforts on and to watch their new leader make a horrible and painful example out of Kritten.

Farnum knew that he couldn't do anything about this. Kritten had betrayed him and now was only using him to try to betray their new leader too. The little piglin likely deserved everything that Uggub was about to do to them.

But Farnum couldn't just watch and let that happen. As mad as he'd been at Kritten for their terrible duplicity, he couldn't just watch them be killed, no matter how appropriate it might be.

Without thinking, Farnum climbed out of the hole and leaped atop the strider once more.

"Go!" he heard Mycra calling in the distance. "Go save them!"

He spurred the strider forward and charged toward Uggub, shouting as he went. "Drop that piglin! Drop Kritten, you brute! Drop my friend!"

Uggub turned toward Farnum and stared at the zookeeper in utter disbelief. No piglin would go to such lengths to save anyone—much less someone who'd betrayed them so badly. To the brute, it just didn't make sense.

That's probably why Uggub wasn't ready as Farnum sped past the shocked piglin and smacked them in the face with his iron shovel.

The attack surprised Uggub even more than Farnum's appearance. They toppled backward, dropping Kritten as they fell, and clutched at their face.

Farnum hauled up short at the edge of the lava pool. For an

instant, he considered going back for Kritten, scooping them up, and riding off with them on top of the strider, but he knew that just getting away wouldn't be enough. He had something else to do first.

Without even getting off the strider, Farnum started digging. At first he went straight down—just far enough to get both himself and the strider underground. The lava began to flow in behind him, and it grew almost unbearably hot. If he'd not been on top of the strider, the molten rock would certainly have burned him to a crisp.

Once he was deep enough, Farnum began digging underground toward the stockpile of obsidian. He worked as fast as he could, moving forward as he went and watching the lava continue to flow in behind him.

By this time, Uggub had recovered from the blow to their face and was snorting loudly enough to shake the walls of the tunnel Farnum was digging. Then, while Farnum continued to burrow through the ground, he heard the sound of digging happening above him, and the roof of the tunnel he'd been digging opened up and let light in.

He glanced back and saw that Uggub had dug their way into the tunnel from above, searching for Farnum and hoping to kill him.

Farnum set to digging with renewed vigor. He knew that if Uggub managed to catch up with him, he'd be finished for sure!

There was always the chance that Uggub would figure out where Farnum was headed and try to head him off before he got there. The only hope the zookeeper had was that Uggub wasn't quite that clever. Not that Farnum had any other options left.

The roof of the tunnel behind him disappeared again, again,

and again as Uggub dug through it, searching for him. Each time, the brute bellowed in disappointment and fury—and each time, Farnum kept digging harder.

As Farnum went, his arms grew more and more tired, and the strider became more scared and harder to control. He knew he couldn't last much longer, but stopping where he was would only mean certain death.

By the time Farnum reached the pit he'd dug beneath the obsidian stockpile, his arms felt like they were made of stone—almost too heavy to lift. When he broke through into the pit again, he almost cried in relief. Despite that, he kept the strider moving, as the lava was still flowing in right behind them!

He heard a mighty snort then as Uggub broke through the ground above once again. This time, though, the brute was no longer staring into the lava-filled tunnel but into the pit!

Seeing the much larger cavity below them caused Uggub to howl in frustration. Perhaps the brute thought that Farnum had found a cave to hide in, which would make finding the zookeeper nearly impossible. Farnum hoped that Uggub would leap down into the pit to see for themself, but the brute was apparently too canny for that.

Instead of waiting for Uggub to figure out a way to reach him, Farnum worked his way around the edges of the pit, knocking out the ceiling above him as he went. He felt like he could barely move his arms, but this was easy going. Rather than chipping away at solid earth, he only needed to remove the layer of gravel overhead so that he could reach the chests above and break them, sending their contents into the lava below.

Farnum had almost gotten all the way around the pit when the ceiling in front of him disappeared! Apparently Uggub had finally figured out the pattern of what Farnum was doing underground and had decided to get in front of him to stop it.

The trouble was that—by doing so—Uggub had taken out the last remaining bit of the edge of the pit's ceiling. Rather than catching Farnum, the brute had knocked out the final bit of the gravel ceiling's support, and the entire roof of the pit plummeted into the lava below. This took with it all of the chests of obsidian that the piglins had brought with them to the Overworld, destroying every last bit of it!

A couple of piglin warriors who had been trying to protect the chests of obsidian tumbled into the lava with them. Farnum felt horrible for them, and given a chance, he would have pushed the strider headlong into the now-lava-filled pit and tried to save them, whether there was wisdom in that or not.

But Uggub didn't give him that chance.

With the roof of the pit entirely gone, the piglin brute could see Farnum clearly now, so they reached down and plucked Farnum straight off the strider's back. The zookeeper had done his best to evade Uggub, but before he could even turn the strider around, he found himself in the piglin leader's grasp.

Farnum struggled as he was lifted in the air, trying to work his fingers in beneath Uggub's meaty hand and pry himself loose. Uggub was just too big, too fast, and too strong, though, and no matter how hard Farnum tried to work his exhausted arms, he couldn't prevail.

If he'd had forever, Farnum might have been able to figure something out, but Uggub cocked back their arm and tried to hurl the zookeeper into the lava, which would have meant certain death. Somehow, with the last of his strength, Farnum managed to hang on.

Frustrated and furious, Uggub spun around and hurled the zookeeper toward the enclosure in the back of the zoo instead. This time Farnum felt his grip give.

Farnum rolled as he hit the ground, tumbling over and over until he smacked up against the gate in front of the enclosure. He hit it so hard that he knocked a hole clean through it.

"Farnum!"

That had to be Mycra's voice, but at that moment Farnum was too stunned to do more than recognize it. The impact had knocked the wind out of him, and it was all he could do to keep his eyes open and look up to see Uggub storming after him to finish the job.

A pair of hands reached through the hole Farnum's landing had created, grabbed him, and hauled him back into the enclosure.

"What?" Farnum didn't understand who had come to help him. "What's going on?"

He looked up to see Mycra holding him in her arms as both she and Grinchard grinned down at him.

Before Farnum could even say thank you, Uggub slammed right into what was left of the gate and began tearing their way through it.

THE FINAL BETRAYAL

The gate to the enclosure nearly gave way under Uggub's ferocious assault, but Grinchard leaped forward to block the brute's path and refused to yield. They put their shoulder against the gate and jammed the edge of their boot against the base of it, and even the massive piglin's shoving against it wasn't enough to get them to move more than a few inches.

"Give me a hand here!" Grinchard shouted to the others, who'd been gaping at their bravery in awe. "I can't hold this much longer on my own!"

Mycra dropped Farnum and dashed over to add her strength to Grinchard's. Uggub smashed against the gate a second time, and the two people resisting the brute's effort both howled out in pain.

That noise got Farnum moving again. He stood up still wondering where his feet were and found them flapping around underneath his knees. Armed with that knowledge, he tottered over toward the gate and—rather than throwing himself—fell against it.

Uggub hurled their bulk against the gate a third time, sending Farnum's teeth rattling.

The zookeeper didn't see how this was going to end well. He thought that maybe he could dig an escape tunnel like he had before, but when he looked down at his hands he didn't see the shovel there. He must have dropped it when Uggub had tossed him aside.

He remembered then about the tunnel that he'd already dug out of the enclosure, and he staggered over toward it. When he reached it, though, he saw that it had filled up with lava that had flowed into it from the lava-flooded pit. That way was sealed off for them too.

To Kritten's frustration, the Great Bungus had taken a bit of convincing just to get the massive piglin back up on their one good foot. The injury they'd sustained from the lava pool still had them in agony, but if one thing burned even stronger in Bungus than the end of their leg it was their desire for revenge.

Once Kritten had managed to slap Bungus back to consciousness, all the advisor had needed to do was point the wounded giant in the right direction.

"There they are," Kritten had whispered to Bungus. "Uggub is right there before you, wounded and distracted and with their back to you. You'll never have a better chance to attack them. If you wait for them to be done with the Overworlders, they're sure to finish you off at their leisure. They might not even bother to dirty their hands with you. Just have the others roll you over into the lava instead."

The prospect of both getting revenge and avoiding a nasty death had prodded Bungus to push aside the horrible pain they were in and mount their retaliation against Uggub then and there. As Bungus lumbered over to take a last desperate shot at Uggub, Kritten stole away and disappeared into Farnum's home.

From where Farnum stood in the enclosure, he could see that Kritten hadn't been idle while Uggub had been chasing him down and trying to kill him. In fact, the advisor had spent most of the time doing something that might not have seemed all that wise at the time but now turned out to be vitally important: waking up Fungus.

The gigantic piglin with the burned-off leg had been crawling up behind Uggub the entire time that the infuriated brute spent trying to smash down the gate. He was still a ways off, but the other piglin warriors had spotted their former leader by now and had taken to snorting and grunting about it to raise the alarm, pointing at Fungus and gaping at them as if the deposed leader had risen from the dead.

Uggub grabbed the gate to the enclosure at this point and, rather than trying to knock it over onto Farnum's friends, seemed like they were about to tear it off its hinges. Just as they were starting to put their legs into it, though, the raucous hubbub the other piglins were raising finally got Uggub's attention, and they looked back to see Fungus lumbering at them.

The sight of Fungus stumping their way toward them on a still-smoking leg—armed with nothing more than sheer wrath and determination strong enough to overcome their agonizing injuries—shook Uggub, but the traitor wasn't about to just hand back the leadership of the piglin invaders. Instead Uggub let go of the gate, turned around, and squared off against the massive piglin they'd betrayed, ready to finish them off for good.

Farnum rushed over to his friends, his head growing clearer by the moment. They all looked better than when he had left them before.

"I got us patched up as best I could," Mycra said. "Grinchard is tougher than they look."

"As are you!" said Grinchard. "If not for you, I'd still be out cold."

An earsplitting snort ended their conversation, and they turned to see Uggub charging straight at Fungus. The traitorous brute would normally have stood a head shorter than their old leader, but with the bigger piglin's ruined leg, Uggub looked down on them now.

Fungus braced themself for the impact, but Uggub lowered their skull and smashed it right into Fungus's chin. The impact knocked Fungus flat over onto their back, and Uggub leaped on top of them, pressing their advantage.

The rest of the piglins stood aside, none of them apparently clear on whom they should be rooting for. Farnum had no doubt that they would cheer for whoever emerged from the fight victorious, and they would pretend that they had been rooting for them the entire time. Meanwhile, they wouldn't interfere, satisfied to merely watch and enjoy seeing the two most powerful piglins around battle each other to the finish.

"What should we do?" Grinchard asked. "One of them is going to eventually win, and then they're going to come after us."

"Maybe they won't," Farnum said with a hope he didn't really feel. "They were content to let us just sit here before."

"Before you escaped, and before we woke up," Mycra pointed out. "Things have changed."

"There's no other way out of this pen?" Grinchard glanced around, hoping to prove everyone else wrong.

"Not unless you're hiding a shovel somewhere," Farnum said. "I mean, *another* shovel."

The three of them all glanced at one another and shook their heads.

Once inside Farnum's quarters, Kritten turned the place upside down, looking for the diamond pickaxe they had coveted since the first official obsidian-for-animals deal they'd made with Farnum. The obsidian had been crucial to their plans, of course. With it, they could build their own obsidian portals from the Nether to anywhere they wanted piglin forces to appear in the Overworld.

But the diamond pickaxe gave them control over those portals. Not only could they build them, but they could then also shut them down.

Bungus and Uggub and all the rest of the piglins might not have considered that angle, but Kritten had. And now was the time to put that part of their plan into action.

Now that Farnum had destroyed all of the piglins' stockpiled obsidian, Kritten knew that they couldn't just build a new obsidian portal to get back into the Nether. There was only one way for them to return home—the obsidian portal in the back of the zoo—and to ruin that for them, there was only one tool: the diamond pickaxe.

Despite not understanding much of what Farnum and his friend Mycra had said about the pickaxe, Kritten found it quickly. It hadn't been hidden so much as tucked away. When the advisor picked it up and hefted it in their hands, they felt compelled for a moment to admire it, not for its amazing utility but for its incredible beauty.

A bellow from Bungus put a sharp end to that moment, and Kritten realized that not much time was left to them before Uggub and the rest of the piglins would come searching for the advisor. When that happened, the chance for their perfect escape would come to an end.

So Kritten sprinted out of Farnum's home, straight for the obsidian portal, the diamond pickaxe firmly in their hand. They glanced over to see what was happening between Bungus and Uggub and saw that their old friend had been beaten flat onto the ground. It would only be a matter of moments before Uggub finished them off.

"We could just make a run for it," Mycra said. "The gate's half broken. We're not locked in anymore."

"And the piglins seem pretty occupied with the big battle going on right now."

As if to punctuate that statement, Fungus found an opening to poke Uggub in the eye, sending the brute squealing and clutching at the injured orb. This was the first good blow that Fungus had gotten in, and it seemed like it might turn the fight's tide.

"That was a cheap shot," Farnum said.

"It's a duel to the death, not a sparring match," Grinchard said. "There's no such thing as cheating when it's your life on the line."

"And probably not at any other point for the piglins," Mycra pointed out. "They don't seem to care much for the concept of honor."

"So, are we going to make a break for it or not?" Farnum asked nervously. His legs were itching to run, but as battered as he was, he didn't know if he could outpace any of the piglins in a foot race.

"I say we stay here," Mycra said. She wasn't looking at the others, though, or at the brutal fight taking place before them. She had her attention fully focused at something else happening beyond the big battle. "We're not going to outrun them. More to the point, we're not going to outrun that."

"What are you talking about?" Farnum stepped over next to Mycra and craned his neck to see what she was gazing at.

There in the distance, Kritten had emerged from Farnum's personal quarters, the part of the zoo's complex where regular visitors weren't allowed. Farnum had wondered where the little piglin had gotten off to after rousing Fungus and sending him back to battle Uggub. He wouldn't have blamed them if they'd simply stepped through the obsidian portal and disappeared into the Nether forever.

Apparently that was still a part of Kritten's plan, as that's exactly where they were heading. With all the other piglins focused on the titanic duel taking place before them, none of them had noticed Kritten moving off before, and they were even less likely to pay any attention to them now.

But Farnum saw then why those piglins had all made a terrible mistake.

"Kritten has the diamond pickaxe!"

Mycra nodded. "The little traitor must have found it right where I told you it would be. They might not be able to speak our language, but I think they've got a better handle on understanding it than we might have guessed."

"What is that little piglin pal of yours going to do with that?" Grinchard said, still a little groggy. "Steal all of the obsidian?"

Farnum chuckled at that. "I already destroyed all of that. There's no more obsidian left!"

"Other than what makes up the portal," Mycra pointed out.

One of the piglins on the far side of the battle finally spotted Kritten and gave the little piglin a mean stare. No matter who won the battle, it was clear that Kritten had run out of friends among their people.

"Hey!" Farnum picked up a rock and tossed it at the staring piglin. It didn't hit them, but it came close enough to draw their attention. "Hey, over here!"

The piglin glared at Farnum, but they didn't move in his direction. That would have involved trying to skirt around the fight, which had drawn closer to the enclosure's gate.

Farnum picked up another rock and threw it at the glaring piglin. This one caught them in the leg and elicited a high-pitched squeal of offense.

That brought a smile to Farnum's face, but it evaporated when the rest of the piglins all turned to see what the problem was. When they did, they saw the glaring piglin hopping around and holding its injured leg. But they also looked past that one and saw Kritten sneaking off behind them.

Even Uggub saw this as he paused from beating up Fungus. Given another moment, the smaller piglin would probably have put a permanent end to the larger one, but when they spotted Kritten skulking away, they shoved themself away from Fungus and started bellowing at the little piglin.

Kritten froze for an instant, perhaps hoping that all the commotion couldn't possibly be focused on them, but that turned out to be pointless. An instant later, every one of the other piglins—besides Fungus, who was too battered to move—rushed at Kritten, snorting and squealing for their blood.

"Run!" Farnum shouted.

The sound of the zookeeper's voice shocked Kritten into action. They turned and fled away from the other piglins as fast as their little legs would carry them.

"They're not going to make it very far," Grinchard guessed. "And they're not going to last very long after they get caught."

"They might make it through the front gates of the zoo in time," Mycra said. "After that, who knows? Maybe they can get lost in the dark?"

"They're not going for the gates," Farnum said.

"What?"

Farnum shook his head, but he never took his eyes off Kritten's progress toward their actual goal. "They're going for the obsidian portal!"

A moment later, Kritten plunged through the portal's field of swirling purple and disappeared. Some of the piglins close to the portal slowed up, unsure if they should try to follow the little piglin back to the Nether or not.

"What good's that going to do them?" Grinchard said. "They're not any more likely to get away in the Nether than they would here, right?"

"You saw what they were carrying, right?" Farnum couldn't help but smile about it.

"My most precious diamond pickaxe," Mycra explained to Grinchard.

Grinchard was mystified by how Mycra was taking the theft of her precious pickaxe. "And you're happy about that?"

"About that? No. About what's going to happen next, if that little traitor is fast enough? Very much so."

The rest of the piglins were getting close to the obsidian portal. A few of them were almost close enough to touch it when the purple field that had been swirling inside of it stuttered and went out, leaving nothing inside it but air.

The piglins all hauled up short, Uggub included. The brute began grunting out orders of some sort, trying to get the piglins to figure out a way to get the obsidian portal restarted. They fired arrows at it. They threw axes at it. They smashed it with whatever they could find.

Nothing worked. The frame remained empty.

Uggub snorted in absolute frustration, and the rest of the piglins—including even the half-conscious Fungus—joined in with them, raising a horrifying chorus of anguish.

TO RULE THE NETHER

Kritten's plans had worked out better than they ever could have hoped when they'd first gotten banished from the bastion. It had been bad enough that the Great Bungus had lost all faith in them, but the fact that they couldn't count on anyone else in the bastion to stand up for them had shattered any other plans they might have had. When the advisor had left the bastion, the only thing they'd hoped for had been to figure out some way to survive the night. That would have been enough of an accomplishment to start with.

Now? Now they realized that *they* could be in charge. No more being the power behind the throne. They would sit on the throne themself.

How would they do that? In piglin society, people followed those who had power, mostly of the physical variety. The larger you were, the better the chance you would be in charge and stay that way.

Kritten had never fit that mold, so now it was time to forge a new one.

It never would have been possible if they'd not been able to get rid of Bungus, Uggub, and all of the best piglin warriors that stood behind them. And none of that would have been possible if Kritten had not met Farnum.

The advisor smiled as they thought about that fateful encounter with the terrified zookeeper so far under the surface of the Overworld. Both of them had been at what were likely the lowest parts of their lives, but they'd risen a long way from there.

Or at least Kritten had.

Farnum's fate would be his problem, not theirs. They'd done everything they could to help him out. Far more than any other piglin would have dared.

Of course, all of those actions had helped Kritten too. They'd just been sharp enough to understand that at the time.

The whole plan might have fallen apart if Kritten had ever showed Bungus or any of the other piglins how to ignite an obsidian portal. Or how to put one out.

The moment they'd entered the Nether, Kritten had turned around and extinguished the portal. Then they'd destroyed the entire thing with the diamond pickaxe, one block of obsidian at a time.

It didn't take long to remove one piece of it, ensuring the piglins following them were trapped on the other side. Just in case someone on this side managed to find a stray piece of obsidian to help them rebuild the portal, though, Kritten kept chipping away at the frame until they'd destroyed the entire thing.

Only then did they allow themself a moment to sit down and catch their breath. They slumped against the spot where the obsidian portal's frame had just been, the diamond pickaxe in their lap, and they took a moment to collect their thoughts.

Then they let out a wild whoop of triumph!

Kritten had gone through the worst time of their life, and they had emerged victorious. Now nothing stood in their way!

The advisor marched all the way back from the remains of that obsidian portal to the Great Bungus's bastion. When they got there, they walked in through the front gate, tall and as proud as they had ever been. The guards there goggled at Kritten, shocked to see them return without any of the other piglin warriors or leaders who'd gone off to conquer the Overworld.

"What happened to them?" one of the guards finally dared to ask as Kritten strode past them. They had to follow the advisor into the bastion to hear the answer.

"They failed at their ambitions and were defeated! I, however, was not!"

Both the guards trailed after Kritten as they worked their way through the bastion to the throne room. Others who spotted them joined them, curious about what was going on. By the time the advisor made it to the throne room, they had a full procession of piglins following in their wake.

With no one to stop them, Kritten climbed into the Great Bungus's throne and sat down. They wriggled around for a moment until they felt comfortable enough and then gazed out at all of the piglins who had assembled there before them to see what was up.

"The Great Bungus is dead!" Kritten said. *Or at least close enough to it.* They waited for the gasps from the crowd to die down and then spoke again.

"Uggub—who betrayed the Great Bungus—is also dead, as are all of those who went with them into the Overworld!"

This caused even more of a hubbub in the crowd as the remaining piglins realized how much they as a people had lost: not just their two most powerful leaders but also the greatest of their warriors. What would happen to them all now?

Kritten had a plan for that.

"I am now in charge here! We have tried the way of brute force and simple muscle, and it has failed us! What we need are intelligence and strategy and wisdom, the kind of wisdom that can guide us through the horrors of this stunning loss and help us aspire to even greater heights!"

One of the guards from the gate stood closest to Kritten, and they were brave enough to ask the question on the mind of every other piglin in the room. "Why should it be you who leads us?"

Kritten had anticipated this. They pulled out the diamond pickaxe and struck the guard on the head with it. As the injured piglin reeled away, the advisor stood up in the center of the throne and said, "Because I know the secrets of the Overworld! I know how to get there! I know how to protect us there! And I know how to conquer it!"

The poor piglins—already shocked by the loss of so much of their people's strength—were cowed by Kritten's declaration and their show of strength. They had never seen such an amazing weapon before, and they were unsure how to stand up to it, much less to the advisor holding it.

Then the other guard who had allowed Kritten to stroll into the bastion started up a chant. "Hail the Great Kritten! Hail the Great Kritten! Hail the Great Kritten!"

The other piglins close by joined in, and then more and more piglins, until soon the entire throne room—and then the entire bastion—rang with the chants of every piglin around.

"Hail the Great Kritten! Hail the Great Kritten! Hail the Great Kritten!"

The advisor—the ruler—of the bastion held their diamond pickaxe over their head in triumph, thrusting it into the air every time the crowd called their name.

As the bastion's newly minted ruler, Kritten wasn't sure exactly how they would manage to conquer the Overworld, but they swore to themself that they would dedicate every ounce of their smarts and of their fellow piglins' power to making that happen. One day—and someday soon—the Overworld would tremble beneath their marching boots, and the creatures who lived there would be chanting Kritten's name too.

LAST CHANCES

When Uggub and the rest of the piglins were done squealing about Kritten's utter—and incredibly successful—betrayal, they all turned their attention back toward Farnum and his friends. Their rage had to be focused on something, and it seemed like the creatures trapped in the unused enclosure were doomed to serve that purpose.

Uggub returned to the gate and put their massive hands on the bars there, ready to finally tear it off its hinges so that the brute and the rest of the piglins could storm into the pen and kill everyone in it. As Farnum gazed up at Uggub, though, he saw not only fury on the brute's face but abject terror.

The brute noticed that Farnum had recognized this in them, and Uggub fell to one knee and struggled with trying not to tremble in fear.

Farnum let out a long sigh. "They're dead," he said to his friends. "Kritten just killed every one of them."

"Are you sure?" Mycra said, far more concerned that the

three of them were about to be killed than with the fate of their attackers.

"They don't have any more of the potion with them here that allows them to survive outside of the Nether. And they have no way to get back to the Nether before the potions they did take wear off. It's only a matter of time before they all keel over and die, just like the hoglin did."

Grinchard swallowed. "And then return as zombies like the hoglin did too?"

"We can't just wait them out here," Mycra said. "We don't want that many zombified piglins wandering all over town."

"We could just reignite the obsidian portal for them," Farnum said. "That would allow them to go home."

"And then come back here and invade again whenever they like," said Grinchard. "Don't you dare."

"We're just lucky they haven't been able to figure it out themselves," Mycra said. "Otherwise, we'd already be dead."

As the horror of that notion grew in Farnum's heart, he realized there was another way. Maybe. He just needed to get Uggub to listen to him.

"I have an idea." He walked toward the gate and waved gently at Uggub to get the brute's attention.

"Please tell me you're not going to save them," Grinchard said.

"I don't know," Farnum said. "But I'm for sure not going to save them here."

Uggub spotted Farnum and responded by rattling the gate and letting loose a savage snort that hit the zookeeper like a hurricane-force wind. Farnum didn't let it cow him. He couldn't afford that.

"I know what Kritten did to you!" Farnum shouted at the brute, hoping they could figure out what he was saying. When he said

Kritten's name, a vicious glint of recognition flared in the brute's eyes.

Farnum mimed himself choking to death on poison and falling over. Under other circumstances, Uggub might have been amused at such silliness, but the sight of the fate that time had in store for the brute and the rest of the piglins instead plunged terror into their heart.

Now that he had Uggub's full attention, Farnum held up a hand and mimed an obsidian portal. Mycra saw what he was doing and helpfully walked right through the imaginary doorway that Farnum had framed out. When she got to the other side, she breathed easy and free.

Uggub grunted at Farnum and pointed at the empty frame of the obsidian portal that Kritten had left through. There would be no escape through that.

"True!" Farnum said equitably. "But that's not the only obsidian portal you know of, is it? There's another one out there."

He arched his eyebrows and raised his voice as he mimed crawling underground and finding another obsidian portal and reacting with relief and delight. Then he turned to Uggub for the kind of response he really hoped would be coming.

The brute stared at him and blinked several times. It took Uggub a long moment, but they eventually got there. Farnum could see the spark of that idea finally catch fire in the brute's eyes.

Uggub cocked his head as if they were thinking, and Farnum guessed he knew what the piglin was contemplating. Did the piglins here have enough time to make it to the other obsidian portal—the one in that watery cave—or was it already too late?

Farnum shrugged at the brute. "I don't know, but do you really have any other choice? It's either give it a shot or die." He knew the piglin couldn't understand his words, but he hoped the sentiment came across.

Uggub let go of the gate and backed up from it, looking defeated but far from done. The brute gave Farnum a grim nod and pointed at the zookeeper and then at the exit to the zoo.

Farnum's eyes grew wide as he realized what the brute was trying to say to him. "They want me to lead them to the obsidian portal."

"That sounds like an awful idea," Mycra said.

Grinchard agreed. "I can't think of any good reason why you'd want to help save any of their lives after what they did to us and the rest of the town today."

Mycra grunted at that. "Well, there's always the other option they have, which is to spend what time they have left trying to kill us all."

Farnum chuckled at her low-key delivery. "Good point." He gazed up at Uggub and nodded. "I'll show you where it is."

"Are you out of your mind?" Grinchard glared at the zookeeper for a moment, then seemed to think they'd figured out something clever. "Are you really going to guide them to that obsidian portal, or are you just going to lead them out into the middle of nowhere?"

"That thought had occurred to me," Farnum confessed as he walked through the gate. "It would be better than letting them run amok in town, for sure. But yeah, I'm actually going to show them to the obsidian portal. Or at least to the tunnel I dug that leads to it."

Grinchard fell in line behind Farnum, as did Mycra. "But why? You know they wouldn't do that for you. Piglins never show mercy of any kind."

Farnum led his friends right through the center of the piglin warriors. None of the invaders even gave them a mean glare. They just bowed their heads and grunted softly as they passed by instead.

"I'm not going to hold myself to their standards," Farnum explained. "I wouldn't have attacked their home either. Maybe this can teach them a lesson about kindness."

"And if it doesn't?" Mycra asked.

"Then maybe it can teach me one instead."

The others could only nod at that. Farnum glanced around the zoo one last time to make sure everyone was ready to go. As he did, he spotted Fungus lying unconscious on the ground.

"What about him?" Farnum said, pointing at the piglins' former leader.

Uggub sneered at the downed creature in disgust. Farnum wasn't about to just abandon Fungus there, though. Not if he could help it.

He led his friends over to Fungus to rouse them. The ex-leader managed to get to their knees, but that was the best they could do.

"They'll never make it to the other obsidian portal like this," Mycra said. "And they're too big for the other piglins to carry them."

"We can't just leave them out here," Grinchard said, then waved off the happy look Farnum gave them. "No, I mean, we can't let them just wander off through town, right?"

Fungus had listened to all of this, and they clearly knew what Farnum and his friends were talking about. Instead of insisting that they take them along, the injured ex-leader crawled over to the empty enclosure and shut the gate behind themself.

"Can we really just leave them there like that?" Mycra said.

"Of course not," Farnum responded. "We need to seal them in."

With no ceremony, Farnum sealed the gate, which had held up admirably, even under Uggub's most forceful efforts. While he did this, Mycra hunted around for Farnum's iron shovel and found it. Miraculously, it was still intact.

Fungus didn't object to being sealed into the pen. They just waved Farnum off the moment the work was done and then collapsed on the softest bit of ground they could find.

"I think we're ready," Farnum said. He walked out of the front gate of the zoo, lit a torch, and began hiking into the darkness.

They had a long way to go, but he knew that time was short for the piglins. He had no idea how short it might be, so if he could have run the entire way he would have, but he had to pace himself or he was sure to collapse.

"I don't think we're moving fast enough for Ugly Bub," Grinchard said, pointing a thumb back at Uggub.

"I can see why they'd be eager to move faster," Farnum said as they trotted along. "But this is about the best pace I can maintain."

Uggub strode forward on their long legs, scooped Farnum up before he could protest, and set the zookeeper on their shoulder. They then set off at a blazing gait, daring the rest of the group to keep up with them.

As they went, Farnum guided Uggub by pointing out the proper path, and the brute immediately obeyed. Some of the piglins fell away as they raced along, but Uggub refused to slow down for them. Mycra and Grinchard stayed behind with those piglins to take up the rear, prodding them to hustle along as best they could.

Eventually they reached the top of the tunnel that Farnum had made leading up from the obsidian portal that he'd found in that underground cave. He clapped Uggub on the shoulder and pointed at it, and the brute set him down next to the open hole.

Farnum pointed at Uggub and then at the hole with both arms. This was as far as he was willing to lead the piglins.

Uggub had started to turn a little green by this point. Otherwise, they might have wanted to argue about Farnum's decision. Instead, Uggub plunged into the hole, trying to race to the bottom of the tunnel before they succumbed to the illness.

The rest of the piglins followed after Uggub one by one, squealing and grunting as they went. Some of them knocked others over in their eagerness to escape, but they all kept moving until every one of them had dived into the tunnel and disappeared.

Farnum pointed at the hole to suggest something, but Mycra was already on it. Using Farnum's iron shovel, she sealed off the tunnel, making sure that at this point none of the piglins could change their mind.

"I can't believe we did that," Grinchard said, shaking their head in disbelief. "What if they survive and come back to hurt us?"

Farnum shrugged. "We know they're out there now. Next time we'll be ready for them. Us and the rest of the town." He had no better answer.

"They didn't look so good anyhow," Mycra pointed out. "That problem might solve itself."

"They might make it back to the Nether in time," Grinchard guessed. "But there's no way to be sure."

Farnum agreed to that with a sigh as he turned and began to lead his friends back home. "Hopefully, we'll never have to find out."

Dawn was breaking by the time the three of them got back to town. The rest of the townsfolk were already out and about, cleaning up the mess the piglins had made and tending to the injured. The invaders had done a terrible amount of damage in the short time that they'd been there, rampaging about the place, but it seemed—to Farnum at least—that his neighbors had all survived.

Farnum would have to explain everything that had happened—and his involvement in it—to the whole town at some point, but he wasn't quite ready to tackle that duty right now. Instead, he led his friends back into the zoo so that they could grab a much-needed rest.

When he entered the place, he heard a horrible low moaning that seemed to reverberate around the entire zoo. He suspected what it might be the moment it reached his ears, and he headed to the enclosure where he and his friends had been held prisoner to confirm it.

Inside, he saw that Fungus had succumbed to the poisoning that the Overworld inflicted on piglins who left the Nether. Kritten's potion that protected them from that had worn off, although it was impossible for Farnum to tell when. He just knew that Fungus as they had known them was no more.

But also that they were still moving around and making all that groaning.

"That there is the biggest zombie piglin I've ever seen," Grinchard said, their mouth in a wry twist. Mycra nodded in agreement.

Farnum hadn't seen nearly so many undead creatures like this, but he could only agree with his well-traveled friends. Fungus was just as big now as they had been in life—with the exception of their burnt leg, of course.

"How is it that Fungus now seems a lot less threatening than they did when they were breathing?" Grinchard asked.

"For one, they're no longer trying to lead an invasion," Mycra said. "For two, they're just groaning now rather than bellowing at the top of their lungs. And for three, they're trapped in that enclosure, right? Right?"

It took Farnum a moment to realize that Mycra had asked him a question. "Right!" he said. "We built that thing to hold anything we might find. Large zombies included!"

Grinchard just kept staring at the undead Fungus and shook their head. "That's good to know, but what now?"

"What do you mean?"

Mycra gave Farnum a good-natured elbow in the ribs. "They mean, *what are you going to do with them?*"

Farnum's face broke into a wide and excited smile. "Oh, that's easy! I'm keeping them! You're looking at the latest and greatest addition to the zoo!"

ACKNOWLEDGMENTS

Many thanks to Nate Crowley for all his inspiration with the story, to Alex Davis for his incredible editing work under sharp pressure, to Elizabeth A. D. Eno for designing such a gorgeous book, and to the rest of the Del Rey team for always working so hard to make these books the best they can be. Thanks also to Alex Wiltshire for his thoughtful and sharp input, and to my many other friends at Mojang for making such wonderful games for us all to enjoy.

Keep crafting.

ABOUT THE AUTHOR

MATT FORBECK is an award-winning and *New York Times* bestselling author and game designer with over thirty novels and countless games published to date. His projects have won a Peabody Award, a Scribe Award, and numerous ENNIE and Origins awards. He also runs the Diana Jones Award Foundation, which celebrates excellence in gaming. His latest work includes Hard West 2, Warhammer 40,000: Tacticus, Marvel Multiverse Role-Playing Game, and the *Shotguns & Sorcery 5E Sourcebook* based on his novels.

He is the father of five, including a set of quadruplets. He lives in Beloit, Wisconsin, with his wife and a rotating cast of college-age children.

Forbeck.com
Facebook.com/forbeck
Twitter: @mforbeck
Instagram: @mforbeck

ABOUT THE TYPE

This book was set in Electra, a typeface designed for Linotype by W. A. Dwiggins, the renowned type designer (1880–1956). Electra is a fluid typeface, avoiding the contrasts of thick and thin strokes that are prevalent in most modern typefaces.